KILLER, KILLER, KILLER

THE DRUG EXCHANGE DEALER

KILLER, KILLER, KILLER

&

THE DRUG EXCHANGE DEALER

CHARLES ANTHONY JACKSON

Ordering Information:

For orders and inquiries, please contact:
1-888-404-1388
www.goldtouchpress.com
book.orders@goldtouchpress.com

Printed in the United States of America

CONTENTS

KILLER, KILLER, KILLER THE DRUG EXCHANGE DEALER

As stated on the W.E.B, there are numerous types of recreational drugs: Alcohol, Alkyl Nitrite (Poppers), Amphetamines (Speed), Anabolic steroids, Caffeine, Cannabis (or Marijuana), Cocaine, and Crack. The main categories are: Stimulants (e.g. cocaine), depressants (e.g. alcohol), opium-related painkillers (e.g. heroin), hallucinogens (e.g. LSD). This is the story of Anthony's debacle with drugs. Anthony's problems might not have been an individual effort but; in conclusion, it was still an oversight for him to realize the situation. A lot of circumstances were either; he was young, curious, or being in the wrong place. In any matter, he was just a victim. Although later in life, Anthony and his associates learned a real lesson from drugs.

Anthony received a phone call from Fungi on his cell phone. Fungi was located at the city bus station in Winston-Salem, NC. Fungi decided to call Anthony and arrange for a meeting at the bus station. Anthony arrived at the bus station. He replied, "What's up Fungi? What's on your mind?" Fungi replied, "Man, I am so glad, you finally arrived at the bus station. I am supposed to do some business with these guys. They want me to hand this briefcase over to them in exchange, I pick up their briefcase. Then, I give this briefcase to some guy for money".

Anthony replied, "Look Fungi, I don't like what you are doing but, hurry up. I am not trying to spend my day off work at the city bus station. I will be waiting in my truck for you". Fungi replied, "Okay, I promise, I want keep you waiting long". Anthony begins to wait in his vehicle. Then, Fungi exits the bus terminal and walks to Anthony's vehicle with a briefcase in his hand. Fungi sits inside Anthony's truck on the passenger side.

Anthony replied, "Fungi is everything okay. Did you get everything squared up?" Fungi replied, "Oh, yea! I just have one problem". Anthony replied, "What is it?" Fungi replied, "I found out; the owner of this briefcase will not be available until tomorrow. I need to stash this briefcase with you in a safe place. Then, I can use the ride home; and I will call you, the next day". Anthony replied, "Sure, what are friends for".

Anthony delivered Fungi to his parents' home. Fungi thanked Anthony for the ride and exited the vehicle. Anthony drives away, before Fungi could enter his house. Fungi notices a red Camaro approaching his driveway at his house. He receives a phone call on his cell phone. The cell phone caller I.D reads Nebraska meats. Fungi answers his cell phone. A man name Tony begins talking.

Tony replied, "My employees have their eyes on you. Do you have my briefcase in your possession?" Fungi replied, "I have your briefcase but, it is not in my possession at this moment. You will receive your briefcase but, there want to be anymore drug exchanges from me again. I am settling the score. Your employees caused to much trouble, to my partner. I don't do business as this". Fungi ended the phone call abruptly.

Next, Fungi calls Anthony and notifies; he is going to get a ride to Days Inn Motel. If Anthony is available, for him to meet there the next morning. Fungi informs; he is in a safe zone, from Tony's drug dealing employees. He will be resting in the motel overnight. Anthony replied, "Fungi, you do not need to be alone in a motel room. You need to be with someone, who you can trust. Please, go back to your parents' house".

Fungi replied, "No! I refuse to go back home. I will take full responsibility because my parents are prominent Black folks in society. Fungi's father was an established bar owner. Fungi's mother was an education teacher at a school. Both parents loved Fungi dearly, among other sons. So happened, Fungi and his older brother would have to be the difficult children. Maybe the stress of having well established parents were the blame.

CHAPTER 1
INTRODUCTION TO FUNGI

Fungi and his older brother were much different than their strict leading parents. Fungi believed; him and his brother were the same. They both dealt in illegal drugs. The daddy also sold drugs but, the difference was he had license to sell alcoholic drugs. Furthermore, they all prospered in selling drugs. Although the mother, she sold pipe dreams, false hope, and fantasies; this what Fungi believed. Fungi figured; a Blackman didn't have a chance in society to survive in the south.

To the end, Fungi loved his parents because they were different than himself. They were successful Black folks in society, who he felt, society was not kind to them. Icons to his fellow race, which he did not want to cause trouble or harm to them. This is the reason; he would do anything to move away. Which is why, he decided to stay in a motel for the night. Fungi wanted to keep his parents safe from harm.

After Fungi checked into the Days Inn Motel, he paid the desk clerk cash for his room. Fungi imagined; this time tomorrow, he would be free from any worries. He would keep the briefcase, he had full of money, despite what Tony wanted. Fungi made plans to divide the money with Anthony because of all the trouble, which was caused. Then, he would move to Washington, DC, as his brother did. Fungi fantasized; it wouldn't be any more problems. It is all over with now.

Intuition told Fungi to walk out of his room balcony glass door and observe, what was outside. Fungi noticed; a red Camaro car was parked in the motel parking lot. He stretched his eyes to get a better look. He replied, "I be damn, Pistol and Bullet are here! I thought for sure, I wouldn't have any more problems". Pistol walked up behind him and replied, "You don't!" Bullet replied, "No more problems for you. Goodbye!". (Then, a loud gunfire of a shooting ammo round sounds off.)

Shortly in time, when Anthony reached his residence, he noticed; his wife Pricilla was on the phone with a life insurance company. Anthony waves, as he passed by her but, not without giving her a kiss on the forehead. Pricilla took a couple of seconds to paused on the phone. She replied, "I am talking to the insurance man on the phone". Then, returned talking on the phone again. Pricilla replied, "Yes, I am in good health. I believe, as I know it".

The Insurance man replied, "Well! We must do a full inspection, to know if you qualify. What we do, is come out unexpected and conduct a routine inspection of your environment. They may not notify you, the first time they come. The inspectors are looking for hazards around your living area. They try to catch by glance, if you are in a good safe condition. If you spot them please, try not to be alarmed".

Pricilla replied, "Well; they can come out and observe anytime they want. I don't work outside the home so; I am mostly here all day. I guess; I will eventually see them soon. Well, goodbye Sir". Anthony replied, "What was this all about?" Pricilla replied, "Not to worry. I am just trying to get some life insurance. Did you pick up Fungi?" Anthony replied, "Yes! Although, the strangest thing happened. Fungi was doing business at the bus station with some guys. Then, the guys trail Fungi out the bus station, watching his every step".

Pricilla replied, "Well; this is not all but strange. Maybe, they wanted to make sure, Fungi departed safely". Anthony replied, "When as Fungi got inside my truck, one of the guys fixed his hand as a pistol and shot at me. Then, they got into a red Camaro sports car, while they smiled". Pricilla replied, "I hope, you told this to Fungi". Anthony replied, "Nope, we only talked about him given me this briefcase to watch until tomorrow morning. Then, he later told me to meet him at the Days Inn Motel".

Pricilla replied, "You should give him a call and tell him". Anthony replied, "I think, you are right". Anthony grabs the phone and dials Fungi. The phone continues to ring without an answer. Then, the voice mail picks up. Anthony informs Fungi to call back. Pricilla replied, "Don't worry, if no one is answering. Fungi will probably be okay. By the way, family from down south, is coming to visit us. Our cousin Angela and her husband Tyrone will be in town". Anthony replied, "I can't believe it. They finally decided to make it up here".

The next morning, there was still no phone call from Fungi. Anthony decided to turn on the news. The T.V. news was reporting a shooting murder at Days Inn Motel in Winston Salem, NC. They announced the victim, as an African American male, slender built in his forties and identified by friends called Fungi. Anthony replied, "Baby come quickly, I must be having a bad dream. The news just reported, Fungi have been murdered in the motel. I can't believe it. I was just with him yesterday".

Anthony informed; please, somebody tell me, I am dreaming. If only he had stayed with his parents, as I requested. Maybe, he would still be alive right now". Pricilla replied, "I can't believe it either. We need to find out, what exactly happened to your friend Fungi; and how did this happen". During the following Saturday, Anthony had two tickets, he had won to the Wake Forest vs Duke College Football game. The game was played in his hometown at Deacon Stadium. Anthony's wife Pricilla had given him permission ahead of time to attend the game.

Pricilla informed; there was one condition although. Anthony had to take his daughter Keke, along with himself to the game. He did not mind because he enjoyed spending time with any of his children. Keke would most likely behave herself until she got restless. She would notify a person ahead of time, before she got tired and restless. If this would not get your attention then, the monster would come out of Keke; and she would start showing out. Anybody, who observed Keke showing out when she was upset, would tell you; it is not a pretty sight.

With Keke attitude changes, there would be cussing, kicking, and biting. It would be just a plain fight on somebody's hand. Sometimes, Keke was a real Dr. Jeckle and Mr. Hyde type of person. Keke would give a warning. Then, she would change into a completely different personality, which would appear inside her. It was an individual's on fault, if they chose to avoid the warning signs. A person would always have to monitor and listen for her behavior.

Anthony prepared for Keke and him for travel to the game. He then, kissed his wife Pricilla goodbye and loaded his daughter Keke inside the pickup truck. When Anthony arrived at the Wake Forest Demon Deacons' Stadium, the parking lot was jammed packed. Keke did not like to walk far away so; he would have to find a close-up parking spot. Anthony searched for about 10 minutes and had no luck finding a close-up parking spot. He replied, "Keke baby, we are going to have a good distance to walk, when we get where we are going because I can't find a close-up parking space".

Keke replied, "Okay". Then, Anthony recognized his co-worker, who was at the game. Anthony's co-worker had finally arrived. He informed; he would be at the main gate. Anthony figured; it would be perfect to meet him there because more parking spaces were available. He exited his vehicle to get a good look at the main entrance. Anthony thought he had located a vehicle, which appeared to fit the description, as the drug dealer's car at the bus station.

Next, Anthony reached his head inside his truck. Anthony replied to his daughter, "I will be right back in one minute. I am going to check something out quickly and fast". Anthony walked up to the drug dealer's car close enough where, he could read the automobile tags. He remembered; the automobile had a scratch on the right-side passenger door of the red Camaro. Anthony thought heavy. He turned around and could barely see Keke getting out his truck, while a stranger was escorting her out the vehicle. Anthony shouts, "No Keke, No! Run away!" He takes off running towards Keke and the stranger.

A taxicab pulls up beside Keke and the stranger. They both got inside the taxicab; and the driver rolls away from the parking lot. Anthony kicked the dirt around the ground; he cannot believe what just happen. He returns to his truck, sits inside and calls his co-worker to inform him about the events, which just occurred. Anthony replied, "Hello Mark, you're not going to believe this but; someone has kidnapped my daughter. I am not going inside the stadium right now. Presently, I am searching for my daughter on the outside.

Anthony reminisces of Fungi. If only Fungi had listened to his brother or him. It all started at an early age in Anthony's life. Anthony was only about 12 years old; and he was looking for the right size Tupperware container to make the perfect bowl of cereal. He realized; his mother kept the bowl size containers on the top shelf in her cabinet. Anthony figured; he would have to grab the stepping stool to reach up on the high shelf to retrieve his favorite cereal bowl.

When he observed his favorite cereal bowl, something in a clear plastic bag, which resemble hay was stashed behind it. Anthony didn't know what it could be. He couldn't imagine, why would his mother have hay in her cabinet? Anthony decided to take the plastic bag down; and it triggered a sense of smell. He never smelled anything, as this odor before. It had a strong odor but; it was nothing like hay. The plastic bag had stems and seeds, which rested at the bottom of the bag.

Also, beside the plastic bag, were some rolling papers and a book of matches to go with it. Anthony immediately returned the plastic bag, rolling papers, and matches, back to its original spot. He closed the cabinet door because he didn't want his mother to find out, he had been in the cabinet. Although, Anthony didn't know, what it was in the plastic bag. He didn't want to get caught noticing it.

On a different day, Anthony decided to play outside in his back yard. Anthony was in the 5th grade Elementary School and learning about science. Anthony's school was teaching reproduction of plants and animals. When it came to flowers, there were 2 types of flowers to learn about. The flowers were perennial and annual flowers. It was during the Springtime so; Anthony was curious to test out, what he had learned, in his mother's flower garden.

Anthony noticed; a flower in his mother's flower garden. He never seen it before. It resembled a wild weed. Anthony thought; this is different because his mother pulls weeds in her garden every week. Then, the following week had passed; and Anthony overheard his brother Jerome talking on the home phone to his brother's friend. Jerome replied, "Hey Fungi! I think, it's ready now".

Jerome replied, "I am going to go outside and cut it down. Then, roll it up in cigars. Fungi, we can smoke a whole entire year with this stuff". The next day, Anthony returned home from school. Jerome and Fungi were having a good time. They were sitting outside, smoking and laughing together. Then, they settled in my mother's basement with snacks.

Jerome was 16 years old at the time and about four years older than, his younger brother Anthony. He was street smart and charismatic. The neighbors' kids loved to associate with Jerome. Anthony was just the opposite. He kept to himself and stayed away from strangers. Fungi was the perfect blend between Anthony and Jerome. He was loud and aggressive. Fungi would tease the neighborhood children for fun and try to influence Anthony to be more outgoing.

CHAPTER 2
IN THE BEGINNING

Fungi was associated with three other siblings. They were all brothers with him being the second oldest. Fungi oldest brother was a member of a drug gang. He was trained and recruited to be a drug exchange dealer, once he reached a legal age. Fungi constantly mentioned his oldest brother's income and valuable possessions.

One day, Jerome was smoking marijuana. Jerome replied, "Man, this is some good stuff. If only, I knew how to sell this without getting caught. I would have so many lady friends, it wouldn't be funny. Then, I would buy me a car and some new clothes". Fungi replied, "There is no way, you could make this happen. You may be smooth with the neighborhood kids but, you are not this smooth".

Fungi replied, "Learn from me because I am the master. You need street friends, as my brother and me. When I get older, I am not going to be like my older brother. Instead, I am going to be better". Jerome replied, "You are going to be a fool. Your older brother got kicked out of school because he never went to class". Fungi replied, "I know all this. Which is the reason why, I am going to be better because I go to class".

Fungi's brother resided in Washington, DC. He relocated to Washington, DC because his mother could not handle the stress of being his parent. Before he relocated, he was able to establish a reputation of becoming a successful drug exchanged dealer in the Winston Salem, NC city area. Also, rumors occurred; he was recruited to do bigger jobs in the Washington DC area. Jerome replied, "Fungi, you need to quit dreaming and leave them drugs alone. Don't strive to be as your brother but, be yourself; or your parents are going to kill you".

Fungi replied, "Hey, don't worry about me and pass me the joint. Anthony was standing right by the basement door, where he could hear Fungi talking to his brother. He had to reposition himself because he began to cramp, standing in one spot for so long. Jerome heard Anthony. Jerome replied, "I hear a little mouse by the basement door. It must be Anthony; or it is about to get smashed".

Anthony replied, "Please, don't hurt me. It is me, Anthony". Fungi replied, "Jerome is this your little brother?" Jerome replied, "Yes; and I am about to send him away". Fungi replied, "Hold on, lets hear what he has to say". Anthony replied, "Jerome, I just want to say hello to your friend". Jerome replied, "Okay, this is my friend named Fungi. This is not his real name but, his nickname because he acts like a fungus, which is hard to go away. It grew on him because he doesn't like to use his real name now anymore".

Jerome replied, "Fungi don't leave on his own. He is never welcome. The only way to get rid of him is you must clean house. I will give a demonstration. Alright everyone, it's late and time to go home". Fungi looked around. Jerome replied, "Fungi, I am talking to you because Anthony lives here. He is already at home". Fungi replied, "Wait a minute. I have something to ask your brother". Jerome replied, "See, I told you. Fungi go ahead and ask."

Fungi replied, "I want to know, if your brother will try this weed out. Jerome replied, "My brother doesn't smoke weed. He is to young". Anthony replied, "I want to try some". Jerome replied, "You don't mean this". Fungi replied, "Please, allow your brother to smoke some so; I can go home". Jerome replied, "Fungi, if you promise to leave, I will allow Anthony to smoke just a little". Fungi replied, "Sure". Anthony took a puff from the marijuana cigarette and began to cough. Jerome replied, "See, I told you. He doesn't smoke. My little brother is too young for smoking"

Fungi replied, "No, he is not. What he needs is guidance and someone, who cares enough to show him the ropes. Anthony try it again but, this time inhale slow and easy. Don't inhale so fast. Then, exhale slowly after you hold your breath for a little while. If you do this, you can get a good contact". Jerome replied, "Alright, since you want to teach Anthony the streets; and he is eager to learn. Then, go ahead and teach him. You just better not hurt my brother; or I will kill you".

Fungi replied, "I am not going to hurt your brother. He is going to be fine." After this incident, an entire ordeal became about. Fungi did not hesitate to show Anthony new ideas from the street. He introduced Anthony to street language, urban games, updated clothes, and neighborhood drugs. It was no secret; Fungi took it personally to school Anthony on urban life.

Jerome decided to have an age seventeen birthday party. During them days, the drinking age in the State of North Carolina was 16 years of age. Jerome decided to buy 2 kegs of draft beer. In one keg, it was filled with Old Milwaukee beer; and the other keg had Old Milwaukee Lite beer. Children in the neighborhood, who were 16 years of age or older, were invited to the party.

A person named Theodore, who was a younger brother of someone there at the party and was not invited, contacted Anthony. Theodore replied, "Hello, Anthony, I know your brother is occupied with his party. I would like to know, will there be beer leftover from the party?" Anthony replied, "Yes, I am most certain, there will be beer leftover from the party". Theodore's brother named Alvin replied, "Please, save my brother and me some. Save me as much, as you can". Anthony replied, "Sure, I will locate some empty milk jugs to store the leftover beer".

Later, when the party ended, Anthony took the remaining beer and poured it in some empty milk jugs. He had four milk jugs filled with beer. When Alvin arrived to pick up the four milk jugs, he was more than pleased. Alvin was so excited; he began to drink the beer, before he got it to his house. Alvin replied, "Wow! This is some good draft beer. Anthony, you should try some".

Anthony began tasting the beer. The beer tasted bitter to him at first but; the more he drank, the better it got. Anthony started to feel different as he drank. He began to feel relaxed and wasn't shy about expressing his opinion. Anthony had just found out, marijuana made him feel good. Now, he realized beer made him feel good also. Anthony replied, "I like the taste of beer and how, it makes you feel".

After this incident, Anthony would drink beer and smoke marijuana on occasions. People would say, "You talked very intelligent, when you are high". During one instance, he was with a guy, who became his friend named Ford. Ford gave somebody money, who was the legal drinking age to buy them beer. Anthony and Ford drank until, they threw up and got sick. This was Anthony's first time getting drunk.

Ford replied, "Anthony, you talked talking intelligent until your speech started to slur; and your voice got loud. Right afterwards, you passed out. The only time, you woke up, was to throw up. I threw up right behind you". Anthony learned from this experience of being intoxicated, it was not a good thing. However, as time elapsed, he began to gain confidence once again with alcohol and drugs.

When Anthony reached high school, he thought; he had become an expert in dealing with drugs. Fungi and Jerome had plenty of discussions with Anthony about drug abuse. Fungi, who was highly experienced with drugs, reminded Anthony; the drugs are only to be used occasionally and not every day. Fungi told Anthony, "I passed by alcoholics and dope dealers every day. This reason is why my brother has been a successful businessman. He is able to influence average individuals in to thinking, they need drugs and alcohol in order to function."

Fungi brother operated a liquor and drug dealing house. Anthony wondered; if he could do the same as Fungi's brother and make a living selling illegal drugs. Why, Anthony wanted to experiment with this idea; he didn't know. It puzzled him tremendously. Anthony had no money to buy drugs or alcohol for sell but; his parents kept liquor and drugs in the house for recreation sporadically.

Anthony's mother kept her entertainment bar stocked because she entertained on occasions. She had a refrigerator designated for cold alcoholic beverages. Jerome grew marijuana recreationally as a hobby and stored it in his bedroom dresser occasionally. Anthony figured; I will just take the items from my family. When, I complete a sell then, I will give them money for the missing items or return the items back.

CHAPTER 3
EASY MONEY

nthony was prepared and excited to try out his drug selling experiment. He drove to school traveling with an installation cooler bag, filled with can beer and a pint-size Ziploc bag of marijuana cigarettes. Anthony had rolled about ten marijuana cigars for sale. He was ready to become a high school drug salesman. Once Anthony arrived at his high school, he notified his friends to tell their classmates; he was selling beer and marijuana by the high school's restrooms.

Before Anthony knew it, there were all kinds of students wanting to purchase drugs from him. Anthony began feeling, as if he was becoming a real drug dealer. By the end of the school day, Anthony had earned enough money to compensate his family for the missing items and earn a reasonable profit. Anthony gave his brother money for the missing marijuana and replaced his mother's beer he took. During the rest of the day, Anthony kept feeling good about himself.

Anthony thought; it was easy to be a drug dealer. When he arrived at high school the next day, there was a school hall monitor present by the high school bathrooms, where he made drug sales the day before.

The school monitor asked Anthony for his school identification. Anthony replied, "Why, what did I do?" The school monitor replied, "I have been ordered to maintain students' conduct by the school's bathrooms because there has been misbehavior around the area a day before."

Anthony wondered; what kind of misbehavior could be going on. Another student told him; they are looking for a drug dealer, who operates by the school's bathrooms. Then, Anthony found out; a student tried to make himself look good by reporting drug use on school property to the school principal. Anthony was so glad; he only wanted to experiment selling drugs for a day. His mother would have never forgiven him, if he had gotten caught selling drugs in school.

Eventually, Anthony told Jerome and Fungi, he made money selling drugs on school property. Jerome was disappointed with Anthony. Fungi replied, "If you are going to be stupid and sell drugs, do it at a place not on school property or around your home. Fungi introduced an area for activities to conduct drug sales. He took Anthony close by a local park area, where students gather to socialize and get high.

Fungi conducted drug sales without Anthony having any clue to what, he was even doing. He stood on a street entrance, before entering the city park area. Fungi wore a long black trench coat because it was on a cold day; and it had plenty of coat pockets. Inside his coat pockets, there were probably 20 small bags of marijuana he stored. Fungi would keep one hand bald up because he had a small sample of a dope bag inside his bald up hand.

Then, Fungi would walk up to an individual, who he felt he could trust going to the park and negotiate a drug sale on a very low-key whisper. Fungi might had spent maybe 2 to 3 hours talking to clients. When Fungi decided to leave, he had sold all his marijuana bags. Fungi confirmed later, he made approximately over 500 dollars within 3 hours to customers going to the park. Anthony was amazed at his expertise in drug sales.

Fungi replied, "Anthony, this is the proper area and technique to conduct a drug sale. As you notice, I am not located at home, school, someone's private, or personal property. I appear to be minding my own business; and I am out, just socializing with acquaintances on the corner. If a policeman happens to appear, I just go my separate ways and come back another day. Always respect the authority".

Anthony and Fungi became good friends. Then, Jerome and Fungi decided to join the U.S Navy. Anthony spent four years at his mother's home address; while Jerome and Fungi grew closer in the Navy together. During this time, Anthony became closer friends to his classmate Ford. Ford was more popular with the girls at Anthony's high school.

Anthony figured; he would mingle with Ford, introduce him to drugs, and show him a good time. In return, Ford would introduce him to some of his girlfriends. At certain events, Ford would invite Anthony to his house. Ford tried to introduce all his girlfriends to Anthony because Anthony had the liquor and drugs, which gave a good party. In addition, Ford knew Anthony would not disappoint him, when he wanted company from a friend. Anthony arrived at every event; Ford gave for his friends.

One day, Ford invited Anthony to one of his house gatherings. Ford notified Anthony; girls would be attending to smoke and have drinks. Anthony could not resist the temptation to show because he enjoyed getting high at parties. He arrived at the gathering in his mother's automobile. Anthony parked the automobile in front of Ford's residence, where females were gathered and getting high. Then, Ford walked outside to greet him.

Anthony had brought beer and marijuana. Then, he noticed; there was a guy mingling with the females. The guy's name was Pete. Pete looked at Anthony's beer and marijuana. He replied, "The marijuana is fine but, women prefer wine instead of beer". Anthony did notice; the girls were drinking, a certain kind of wine. It was cheap wine called Boone Farm.

Anthony had never experience drinking wine before. Pete was clearly having a wine drinking contest. He was trying to entice the females and everybody else to have a wine drinking contest with him. Everyone, who was standing outside while smoking marijuana, joined and started drinking wine. A few people requested to go inside Ford's house and party because he was alone. The girls ended up, wanting more wine.

The girls had drunk the last bottle of wine. Pete replied, "Anthony, I can tell. Ford and you want to impress these girls. They will certainly leave, if there is no more wine. I know, you don't want them to slip away. Ford and you should stay with the girls. I will bring back more wine with your car. It will only take a few minutes because the store where I buy the wine, is only a few minutes away".

By this time, Anthony was intoxicated and not thinking straight. Anthony replied, "Okay, Pete. This is my mom's automobile, I am using. If you be safe and quick, you can use the vehicle". Anthony figured; it probably would be best, if Pete drove anyways because he was a more experienced driver. He couldn't afford to get a D.U.I ticket on his record.

The last thing Anthony remembered; he was watching T.V, smoking a marijuana cigarette, and waiting on Pete to return with the wine. Then, Anthony got sleepy and passed out on Ford's sofa, right in front of the girls. Later, Ford awakens Anthony. Ford replied, "Anthony, you have to go, before my mom return home from work". Anthony didn't know, what was going on.

Ford replied, "Anthony, you need to find out, where Pete has your mom's car located. It is getting very late". Ford was right. Anthony looked outside at the sky; and the sun began rising. Still, there was no sign of his mother's car. Anthony became mad and desperate. He walked all over the neighborhood looking for his mom's car. Then, Anthony decided to give up and return to his home.

Anthony was extremely upset with Pete; he could have killed him. Fortunately, there was no sign of Pete. Tragically, what appeared halfway down the road from his mom's house; located was his mom's car. The car was parked in a ditch on the side of the road. Anthony was ashamed; he allowed a smooth-talking con-artist to persuade him to use his mother's car. Now, he would have to walk home and explain to his mom; he got high while allowing someone to wreck her automobile.

When Anthony finished explaining to his mother about the incident; his mother gave him an ultimatum. She replied, "Anthony, after completion of high school, you have to find a job and move out or sign up in the military. Also, you have the option to attend a college, while living on campus. Either way, you must leave after graduating from high school". Anthony figured; U.S Army was his best option.

Although, Anthony did drugs; he believed, he didn't have a drug problem. Only by accident, was all his problems drug related. Anthony thought; if only he could join the military. He could break the drug epidemic which was motivating him to do drugs. Then, finally he could get his life on the right track. His brother Jerome and Fungi were already members so; he could easily join as well.

Jerome returned from the Navy, and then, Fungi returned also. They tried to explain to Anthony, why the military was such a serious decision. Jerome replied, "The military is a lot of responsibility and sacrifice. A military employee gives up personal time, space, and sometimes happiness to serve in the government. A military employee's job was twenty-four hours and seven days of the week, all year long".

Anthony listened to his brother but; he was unconcern about the worry Jerome and Fungi felt. Less freedom and more responsibility were his last worries. Anthony was more concerned about his relationship with his mother. This was more important to him than any other thing. Overall, he made his finale decision to join the Army and notified his mother. First, he had to pass stipulations, before he could qualify with the military.

When Anthony took the military drug test, he thought all about the beer, liquor, and marijuana in his system. He made a deal with himself; if he passed the test, he would stay clean, his entire military service. The Army recruiter informed Anthony; he must do a better job taking care of his physical health. The Army recruiter reminded Anthony to exercise, eat right, and stay away from drugs. In addition, leave his no-good friends alone because they are not going to help him pass the Army test.

After Anthony was advised by his Army recruiter of right things to do; he momentarily stayed away from drugs and spent more time socializing with his mother. Anthony's mother taught him how to eat right and exercise to lose weight. She was very excited about Anthony's motivation to do right. Within a year's time, Anthony took the Army test and passed. Then, Anthony took the drug test and passed this also. Finally, Anthony was able to join the military after his high school graduation.

While in the military, Anthony enjoyed his life. Anthony enjoyed exercising, staying fit and eating healthy. Quickly, he began to be drug free and was satisfied. Anthony's first duty assignment consisted of living with a roommate named Lancaster. Lancaster was a taller older gentleman, who was military experienced. He replied, "All this extra military exercising, eating healthy and other gun ho' crap, don't do anything. It doesn't make your time feel better. What you need, is a female companion soldier".

Lancaster replied, "My friend and I are invited on a date with some lovely ladies. You can tag along, if you are not too slow. If you are then, drag behind. Look at these female soldiers, who we are dating. They are seeking male soldiers, who got game". Anthony replied, "Sure, I got game". Lancaster replied, "Look, it's no problem, if you don't have game. Just say, you don't have game. We will introduce you to someone, who is fun".

Anthony hesitated for a couple of seconds to pause and think. Then, he replied, "I am going to tell you the truth. I don't have no game". Lancaster laughed. He replied, "It's okay. Just follow my friend and I. We will do everything but; you must keep up with our pace.

Prior to the date, Lancaster's friend Mitchell introduced himself to Anthony. Anthony shook Mitchell's hand.

Lancaster replied, "Between my friend and I, you don't have to ever worry about a female companion anymore". Before they ventured out on a date, Lancaster replied, "My friend and I, we partake in drinking a couple of alcoholic beverages before going out on dates. I hope, you do drink". Anthony was plenty skeptical. He had not drunk alcohol in months since entering the military.

Lancaster replied, "Anthony, why are you looking worried? You don't trust us". Anthony replied, "The last time, I drunk alcohol; I was doing drugs and my mom's car got wreck". Lancaster replied, "Get over it, you are in the military. Let the past be past; besides your mother is not here. You are responsible for your own actions. Live your life kid". Anthony replied, "Alright, before I start drinking, can I get a Goody powder from someone".

Anthony loved Goody's powder pain relief medicine. He made it a habit to take one for prevention of hangovers. It worked fast, in his system. By circumstance, Lancaster acquired a Goody's powder pain medicine for Anthony to swallow. Then, Lancaster, Mitchell, and Anthony decided to drink alcohol beverages until there was a knocking on the door. When they opened the door, women appeared at the front room entrance.

Anthony noticed; three beautiful females entering the room. Mitchell informed Anthony to retrieve some chairs for the beautiful ladies. Anthony returned with some folding chairs for the ladies. The ladies were recalling their past; and how they use to get high on drugs. Anthony became immediately interested in the conversation and sat down beside the women who was talking.

One woman, who was recognized by her nickname New York, spoke with a street slang accent. New York was darker skinned than the other two women but beautiful. It was as if her skinned was the color of coco chocolate but smoothed as a baby bottom. She had straight hair with curls at the end. The woman was flat out gorgeous but controlling.

New York was bragging about how she smoked marijuana; and it made her feel good. Anthony noticed; Lancaster and Mitchell were glazing at each other, as if this woman was a sign from heaven. Anthony became excited because everyone else appeared so interested, listening to the woman's confession. Immediately, Anthony identified her as the leader of the three women.

Another lady interrupted the conversation and informed; she had sniff cocaine. Her nickname was Philadelphia because she was from Philadelphia. Philadelphia was gorgeous as well but in a different way. She wore her hair in a short classic cut style and would inform you every chance of things which was outdated. She was looking for new and improved ideas. Her total mission was to gain recognition above all her peers.

Anthony could tell, Philadelphia believed she was more qualified and wanted to be the best. She replied, "I love doing coke, speed, cocaine because I am not a big drinker. Marijuana is okay too but; the real high is cocaine. I prefer not to waste my time with old things, I have done in the past. Cocaine is what the rich people are doing today. I want to blend in with the rich people". Lancaster and Mitchell appeared to be fascinated by the words coming out of Philadelphia mouth.

Then, the last girl named Tennessee replied, "Now, I have tried alcohol. Although, the things you all are talking about, I have never tried". Tennessee appeared younger to Anthony and slightly above average looking. She reminded him of typical southern woman because she spoke politely. To Anthony, there was no indication Tennessee was wearing any makeup. Anthony thought; Tennessee was just a pure natural pretty girl.

Mitchell replied, "Tennessee, I would have guessed, you would have said this because you are from the south. Therefore, you might not be able to hang out with us". New York replied, "To do drugs make you sin and have sexual encounters". Philadelphia replied, "Do anybody knows where we can get some drugs?" Lancaster replied, "My roommate has drugs. He just tried out some drugs. Anthony use to do drugs every day. He even sold drugs".

Anthony forgot, he told his roommate Lancaster of his story; how he sold beer and marijuana in high school one day as an experiment. Anthony replied, "Excuse me but, I don't have any drugs. Mitchell replied, "Anthony, I think you do have drugs. Ladies excuse us men, while we negotiate on getting some drugs from Anthony". Anthony, Mitchell, and Lancaster step out of the dorm room, into the dorm room hallway.

CHAPTER 4
MILITARY DRUG DEALER

The men began negotiating about drugs. Lancaster replied, "We are going to get some drugs, for these women some kind of way". Anthony replied, "I don't know, how to get some drugs! I am overseas in Korea with the military. I am not in the United States of America". Mitchell replied, "Anthony, you are going to make some cocaine, for these women". Anthony replied, "I don't know nothing about cocaine except; I only seen the movie Scarface, where a man was sniffing some white powder stuff".

Mitchell replied, "Great, what did it resemble?" Anthony replied, "It looked white as sugar but; it made you feel good". Lancaster replied, "Well, we can't use sugar. They would know, it's not cocaine because it is too sweet". Mitchell replied, "Think of something else white, which relieves pain". Anthony thought; he had just taken a Goody's Powder pain killer. It was white, and it made him feel fantastic.

Anthony replied, "Give them the famous Goody's Powder pain killer medicine". He had stashed extra packs of Goody's Powder pain medicine in his front pocket. Anthony took the medicine out his front pocket. Mitchell grabbed the medicine. Mitchell replied, "I think, I have seen the Scarface movie too". I am going to borrow a mirror from someone. Then, I will put the medicine on the mirror in a white line".

Mitchell borrowed a mirror. The guys returned inside the room and joined the women. Mitchell replied, "I knew my friend would have some drugs for everyone. We have some nice cocaine here". The women looked shocked. Then, they got excited. Lancaster snatched the mirror from Mitchell. Mitchell retrieved a little pouch of medicine out his pocket and sprinkle it on the mirror in a straight line.

Mitchell began instructing the women, as if they were in the movie Scarface. He showed them how to take a straw and sniff the powder up their nose. New York tried first. She replied, "Wow! This is some good stuff". Then, Philadelphia tried it. She claimed, "This here is better than what they would have at home in Philadelphia". Tennessee sniff the medicine. She replied, "I feel different. I am getting so hot". Tennessee started removing her clothes off her body.

Mitchell replied, "I think, New York and myself are going to go solo to my room with a little powder". Mitchell winked his eye at Lancaster. He replied, "We are going to take care of some business in my room, while you all handle business here". Lancaster replied, "I got my clue. This leaves me with Philadelphia. I will take a walk with Philadelphia to her room". Lancaster winked his eye at Anthony. He replied, "Tennessee and you have fun. I will be back in an hour".

After Lancaster and Philadelphia exited the room, Anthony noticed; Lancaster had made a homemade petition out of rope and curtains to separate his section of the room. Lancaster had the left side; and Anthony had the right side. Lancaster had already pulled the curtains around his section to obtain more privacy. Anthony informed Tennessee, if she wanted more drugs, he could get some more drugs. Before this could happen, the woman already had begun stripping naked to her underwear.

Anthony became worried; he hoped Tennessee was okay. He could tell Tennessee wanted to kiss him. Tennessee replied, "Come closer to me, where I can hold you". Anthony ventured closer to Tennessee until he overheard Philadelphia outside the dorm door. Philadelphia replied, "Hey! Who do you think, I am? I am not, your prostitute. I not going to allow you to treat me this way".

Philadelphia began knocking on the door and requesting to speak with Tennessee. Anthony opened the door. Philadelphia replied, "Tennessee put your clothes on. Why don't you have your clothes on. Tennessee, it is time to go". Tennessee rushed to put her clothes on. Then, she departed but; as if she was in amazement. Anthony believed; she was disappointed. He thought also; she probably was having a good time because she smiled at him before leaving.

The next day, Anthony decided to pay Tennessee a visit to her room. Anthony did not know; Tennessee and Philadelphia were roommates. When Anthony knocked on Tennessee's dorm room door, Philadelphia opened it up. Philadelphia informed Anthony to come inside her room, if he wanted to talk to Tennessee. It was obvious, Lancaster made Philadelphia upset because Philadelphia was not happy.

As Anthony entered the dorm room for unknown reasons, he believed; Tennessee and he were not right for each other. Anthony figured; Tennessee was a hazard about to happen. How did Tennessee snort some make believe cocaine and decided to get undress? She acted, as if she was high. Although, Tennessee probably had drinks before arriving also. Tennessee was entirely to gullible and unpredictable for him to date. Anthony would only send his regards to Tennessee and Philadelphia. Then, he would leave.

Anthony's roommates Lancaster and Mitchell just had approximately one month left to be overseas. Then, they would be sent back to the United States. During the rest of their time being overseas, they spent partying and getting high. Lancaster began making drug deals with someone back in the United States for shipments of cocaine by mail. When that occurred, Mitchell, Anthony, and he started advertising to every good-looking available woman. They advertised to who they thought would be interested in getting high; they had drugs for sale.

Suddenly, Anthony noticed his health started to deteriorate from doing drugs. Anthony began slowing down from getting high too much. Lancaster and Mitchell continued with their drug use until they departed the country. The word got out before they departed; access to cocaine was somewhere located in the dorm rooms. The Company Commander over the dorm rooms, made a mandatory drug testing. Before this could happen, Lancaster and Mitchell escaped to the United States without getting tested.

In addition, Lancaster introduced his replacement named Bell to his drug connections in the United States. Anthony's new roommate named Bell, started to receive drugs, just as Lancaster did. When Anthony would arrive at his room, he would notice a delivery box at the room door for soldier Bell. Bell would come in the room, grab his package box and head straight for the bathroom. Bell would come out the bathroom within an hour and be happy as a newborn baby.

Occasionally, Bell would forget Anthony was trying to slow down, on doing drugs. Bell would ask Anthony, "Do you want to snort some cocaine?" Anthony would be offended and shake his head, in response to no. At one time, Anthony came home early from work. Bell was in the dorm room on his bed with a curtain petition separating his side of the area. Anthony did not think anything unusual because Bell had done this before, when he decided to sniff drugs.

Unexpectedly, right when he was about to change clothes, Anthony heard a woman's voice through the petition. Anthony replied, "Hello, Hello! Bell, do you have female companion with you over there?" Bell replied, "Oh, yes! I forgot to tell you; my girlfriend is visiting me today". Anthony replied, "Okay! Now, you want to tell me about your friend. Only, when I inquired about it. I need to definitely have a conversation with you privately". Bell pulled his curtain back. The woman and Bell were both naked.

Bell replied, "You can tell, I am very busy at this moment. Don't even think about making a scene because you can't join us". Anthony did not make a response, he kindly grabbed him a tote bag and left the room. He realized; Bell was not going to be a good roommate. Anthony figured; cocaine was taking over Bell's personality. Eventually, Bell started bringing more women over for sex unannounced. It got so terrible; Anthony didn't want to live in his room anymore.

The situation lasted about three weeks. Then, a big guy, who was a weight trainer, knocked on Anthony's room door. He replied, "I am looking for a nice pretty girl about so high named Tasha. She is my girlfriend. They say, she comes here frequently to buy drugs from a guy named Bell". Anthony politely called out Bell's name. Then, he questioned the big guy, "Why are you sure, you said Bell?" Bell was relaxing. He raised up and replied, "Who keeps on calling my name? Did someone say Tasha? Is my baby, Tasha out there now?"

Anthony turned and looked towards Bell. He began shaking his head and whispering, "Bell run". Bell stands up and reply, "Who is asking about my Tasha?" He starts walking out the room door. Clearly, the big guy was a good four inches taller and much bigger than Bell. The big guy was waiting on Bell. After Bell walked out the room, Anthony quietly closed the dorm door behind him. An argument begins. Then, Anthony could hear a scuffle or fight going on.

The last thing Anthony hears was the big guy announcing, "I don't care, who you get; you are going to leave my girlfriend alone". After a few minutes, Anthony hears the military police in the hallway. A military policeman knocks on Anthony's room door. Anthony opens the room door. The military policeman asked, "Excuse me but, are you Bell's roommate? If you are, I would like you to identify Bell's personal property. We need to confiscate everything he owns".

Anthony helped and assisted the military police gather all of Bell's personal belongings together. The military police Informed him; they will take all Bell's property and store it at the military police station. Bell was being charged with fighting and disorderly conduct. Then, later with drug use. Anthony felt sad but, he eventually was relieved because his main problem was cured. Bell started to have a real drug problem.

Now, Anthony had acquired the entire room alone. He wondered; what was he going to do in his room alone? Then, an unsuspected woman knocked on the room door looking for Bell. This woman was someone, he didn't recognize. She was beautiful. Anthony replied, "I am very sorry; but Bell, he doesn't reside here anymore". She was so disappointed; she turned around as if in disbelief. Anthony was confused.

Another lady came looking for Bell. Anthony informed her; Bell got arrested for fighting. The lady reacted by confessing her life was lost because she had no more drug connections. Bell was her only cocaine supplier. It appeared; she was in a desperate need. Anthony felt sorry for her. He wondered peradventure; if he looked around the dorm room, possible the military police mistakenly missed some cocaine left in an undisclosed location.

Anthony told the lady, "If you would leave your contact information, I will get back to you soon. Later, I might will come across some cocaine". The lady replied, "Okay, I will leave you my contact information". After the lady departed, Anthony searched in the bathroom and discovered a small envelope stuck under the sink pipes. Inside the envelope was a clear plastic bag, full of rock cocaine and a contact number for cocaine dealers. Anthony could not believe his eyes.

Anthony notified the lady; he had discovered his roommate's cocaine and where he was getting his drugs. The lady replied, "I will pay you for cocaine because my girlfriend enjoys sniffing coke. Anthony figured; it was fine. She could pick some up, whenever she wanted too. The lady and her girlfriend arrived at Anthony's room door with fifty dollars to buy drugs. Anthony gave them a street value of probably half this amount.

The lady replied, "If possible, can we try it out here". Anthony replied, "Yes but, sniff it in the bathroom in the memory of my roommate Bell". The ladies departed to the bathroom to sniff a sample of the drugs. Anthony began to worry because the ladies were in the bathroom for a long time. He put his ear up against the bathroom door. Anthony could hear one lady making groaning noises. Then, he overheard a lady imply, "Wow, I like how you do me. You must stop; before I explode on your face".

Anthony could not believe it; he heard this. After 30 minutes passed, the ladies eventually opened the bathroom door and walk out. As they passed by him, one of the ladies kiss him on the lips. Then, the ladies informed them; they had a great time in his room. The ladies requested, if they could return another time. Anthony replied, "Sure, I don't see any reason, why you shouldn't come back. After the ladies left, Anthony washed his lips with some soap and water.

The next day, Anthony informed his co-worker name Hunter, the incident with the ladies. Hunter replied, "You should have invited the ladies to a threesome in your room". Anthony replied, "I didn't think these ladies would be freaky. They are very beautiful". Hunter replied, "Next time, you encounter them in your room, ask them on a date. Then, if they say yes, you should probably ask them to participate in a threesome".

Anthony thought about having a sexual encounter with the two ladies. He figured; he should ask the two ladies to participate in a threesome. The main lady, who asked for drugs, was named Melissa. Melissa was standing in the hallway. Anthony asked her, "Do your friend and you believe in threesomes?" Anthony found them very attractive. Melissa replied, "It depends on what the reward would be. Anything can happen, if there is enough alcohol and cocaine involved to get us high".

Anthony thought; here I go again, involving myself with finding drugs, only to experience a threesome with two beautiful ladies. He remembered; his ex-roommate Lancaster and Mitchell bragging about a foreign cab driver and propositioning them with drugs. Lancaster and Mitchell beat the cab driver up. Then, they stole the cab driver's drugs, before they left the country. The cab driver didn't report it to the military police because he was too scared.

Anthony figured; he would ask the same cab driver, where can you buy drugs around town. There was always a cab driver in close distance available. Anthony noticed; a cab right outside by his dorm. He asked the cab driver, "Hey, where can you get some coke?" The driver replied, "I will give, you some coke; if you get me some expensive American liquor".

The cab driver gave Anthony a ride to the liquor store on the military base. Then, he gave Anthony some coke and money for the liquor. The problem was Anthony had to smuggle the liquor off the military base. It was against the law to take American products sold on the military base away from military property while station overseas. To break the law was call black marketing. Black marketing was buying American-made products on base and attempting to sell the product in a foreign country at a higher price.

The military base had a surrounded fenced wall. It was always protected by military police. Anthony informed the cab driver; he would meet him outside the base gate with the American made liquor. He bought a tote bag and used old towels as packing cushion for placing the liquor inside the bag. Anthony carried the bag to a secluded area inside the military fenced wall. He tossed the bag with the liquor inside over the wall, where he hoped no one would notice.

Slowly, Anthony walked to the main entrance exit. Military police were monitoring and exiting the base. The cab driver was waiting for his liquor. Anthony retrieved the bag outside the fenced wall and gave it to the cab driver. The cab driver was very excited and informed Anthony; he can do this, whenever he wanted too. Afterwards, this made Anthony very happy. Anthony finally spent time with the two ladies, who he wanted drugs for.

Anthony spent time with the two ladies in a Motel room. He fell in love with the two women. Anthony became addicted to the women's pampering and attention. Then, his time became short; and he only had thirty days left overseas. Anthony was so infatuated with the two women; he desired one last fantasy night with the two ladies in a motel. In order to accomplish this, Anthony had to obtain more coke.

Anthony contacted the cab driver, who could give him coke. Everything was going fine until he decided to go out the main gate to retrieve his bag with the American liquor inside. Anthony could not find his bag. A military policeman had confiscated his bag. Then, the military policeman tried to arrest Anthony. Anthony ran so fast, he escaped; and people who observed the incident, called him speedy. He was so scared; he didn't venture out the dorm anymore. In his anticipation, he finally became eligible for return to the United States.

Before Anthony departed to the United States, he had one more supply of drugs to last him one night. Anthony quarantine himself in his room and spent the rest of his time with the two ladies. He was sad to leave the ladies but, happy to return home in one peace from overseas. As he made it home, Fungi and his brother Jerome were together doing the usual things. They were smoking marijuana and talking old times.

Fungi began bragging once again, how he was a big timer. He resided for a short time in Washington, D.C close to his brother. Fungi's brother moved to the State of Maryland and sold drugs. All Fungi talked about was how good his brother had it there. Fungi was married; and then, divorced because his wife could not handle his trifling ways. Eventually, he moved back to Winston-Salem, NC.

Fungi and Jerome decided to make plans to visit Maryland. Fungi started implying, "My brother always kept good ganja up there!" Furthermore, they decided to drive to Maryland in order to buy good quality marijuana. Altogether, Jerome, Fungi and Anthony piled in Fungi's Pontiac Firebird automobile. The trip was going fine until Fungi decided to make a stop in Washington, D.C to visit a friend.

Fungi's friend stayed in a row house apartment. During the entire time, Anthony made sure, he kept an eye on the whole front area of the apartment because the stray-walkers there were drinking and cussing. There was one stray-walker even carrying a pistol on his side. Anthony's brother Jerome notice it. Jerome replied, "I don't like hanging around here". Anthony replied, "I am hungry!"

Fungi's friend overheard Anthony mention, he was hungry. He informed Fungi; he would drive Anthony, one block around the corner to get some food. Jerome replied, "If he can keep my brother safe, he can travel to get something to eat". Fungi replied, "Okay, he can ride but make sure, he is taken good care of". Fungi's friend replied, "Fungi quit acting crazy. Nothing is going to happen to him around the corner".

Fungi's friend jumped in Fungi's car on the driver side. Afterward, he told Fungi to give him the automobile keys. Anthony jumped in, on the passenger's side. When Fungi's friend decides to stand straight up, his full height is about 6'foot 3 inches tall. Fungi's friend talked with a deep heavy voice. He wore jeans and a sweatshirt with words which read, "Bad Boys for Life". Also, Fungi's friend carried a pistol in his back pocket. He took it out and laid it between his legs.

Anthony looked at Fungi's friend with the pistol between his legs. Instantly, Fungi's friend replied, "I carry this for emergency backup only. You can never be to careful in an area as of this". When Fungi's friend and Anthony arrived at the deli shop on the corner block, Anthony noticed; a liquor store right beside it and a strip club on the other side. Anthony replied, "How convenient for a Black person to find food, liquor, and entertainment all on one street block. A Blackman's dream".

Fungi's friend opened the automobile door and got out. Anthony did the same. They both entered the deli shop, and there was an Oriental gentleman behind the cash register. Anthony ordered three cold cut sandwiches for Fungi, Jerome, and himself. Fungi's friend ordered a fish sandwich for himself. Fungi's friend and Anthony decided to take a seat and wait for their food.

A few seconds passed, after they ordered their food. About 10 more Oriental gentlemen entered the deli shop and ordered food. Anthony assumed, they were acquaintances with the man behind the cash draw because they were talking, laughing, and appeared to be reminiscing with each other. After the man behind the cash draw, finished taking orders from the last customer, he called Anthony order up.

Anthony paid and retrieved his order of food at the sales counter. He then, returned to his seat. Suddenly, the cash register man skipped Fungi's friend's order and began announcing the 10 Oriental gentlemen's order. Fungi's friend replied, "How did all these short Oriental noodle heads get in front of me? I can't stand them. They are extremely rude, how they all are blocking the counter from everyone else. I can't even make it up there to check on my order because they are standing in the way".

The cash register man observed Fungi's friend becoming disgruntle to the other Oriental gentlemen. He continued calling out food orders, as if nothing was happening. Fungi's friend checked his food receipt order. He replied, "They should have called my order a long time ago. If this cash register man doesn't call my order next, I am knocking every Oriental guy out in this line".

The cash register man continued shouting food orders to customers but, he still didn't call out Fungi's friend food order. Fungi's friend hopped out his chair. He replied, "This is it, I can't take it anymore". Anthony replied, "Wait a minute, you are going to shoot a person over food?" Fungi's friend replied, "Oh, you are right. I almost forgot; my pistol is in my back pocket. Anthony keep my pistol, temporary for me". Fungi's friend runs to the sales counter.

Fungi's friend shout, "Move the hell, out of my way, Oriental noodle heads! I am not going to say it no more". Some Oriental men replied, "What is wrong, with this guy? What is the problem?" Fungi's friend replied, "Where is my food. I want my food now!" The cash register man replied, "It's coming, don't worry". Fungi's friend replied, "Don't worry about it. I will get my own food, from one of these Oriental noodle heads".

An Oriental gentleman tried to comfort Fungi's friend by rubbing him on the back. Fungi's friend turns around and hits him squarely in the nose. The Oriental guy falls flat on his back. Another Oriental guy tries to come for the rescue but; Fungi's friend kicks him in the stomach. Next, Fungi's friend starts to throw punches at every Oriental guy in the deli, who comes close to him. The cash register man runs from behind the sales counter in a panic and hands Anthony the food for Fungi's friend.

Fungi's friend had laid out every Oriental guy in the deli, except the cash register man. The cash register man replied, "Please, stop fighting. I have given your food to your friend. I am going to call the police. You beat up my family and my friends. Please, go home now!" Fungi's friend began grabbing all the Oriental gentlemen's food left on the counter. He informs Anthony; we are leaving. I need your help, taking all the food home.

Anthony was stunned and surprised. He had never seen anyone in person, display such a fighting skill as Fungi's friend. Then, Anthony becomes normal again from being hypnotized from the trauma. While gathering some of the bags of food, Anthony sat it inside Fungi's car. By the time, Anthony returned to the apartment, he begins to shake again. Anthony notices; Fungi and Jerome sitting on Fungi's friend's apartment steps. They were smoking marijuana and drinking beer.

Jerome replied, "What took you all so long? I am hungry now". Fungi replied, "Me too!" A police car came strolling down the road, headed to the deli shop. Everyone stopped and watched. Fungi replied, "There they go!" Fungi's friend replied, "You so crazy man. Pass me that marijuana joint over here. You are going to have to learn, how to share with your friends". Fungi's friend took a long puff on the marijuana cigarette and passed it to Anthony. Anthony's hand was trembling, when he grabbed the marijuana cigarette.

Anthony took his time, smoking the marijuana cigarette. Then, he reached in Fungi's automobile and grabbed the food from the deli shop. Jerome replied, "Thanks for the sandwiches. Good looking out". He noticed; something strange about his brother. Jerome replied,

"You seem a little shaken. You are okay, right". Anthony tried to show, a blank expression on his face. He replied, "Don't worry, I am fine".

Everyone finished their beer and smoking marijuana. Fungi replied, "Anthony and Jerome, we must load up because we have an important package to pick up from my brother. My brother's ganja is waiting in Maryland". Fungi had not spent time with his brother in a long while. He couldn't wait to see his brother again and retrieve his package.

While they were traveling, Jerome witnessed a prostitute in the business district. The prostitute was concealed by the night light. Jerome discovered the prostitute and revealed it to Anthony. Anthony pointed at the prostitute. Fungi observed Anthony staring. He replied, "Watch me pull over and trick her". Fungi drifts to the side on the road and parks his automobile. The prostitute rushes to Fungi's car.

As the prostitute puts her hand on Fungi's car, Fungi rolls his window down. Jerome replied, "How much do you charge? Wait a minute. You look as if you could be a man". The prostitute replied, "I am not a man". Jerome replied, "You bet not be. Let me take a closer look". He stuck his head out the vehicle to get a better observation.

The prostitute walks closer to Jerome. Jerome replied, "Repeat what you just said again". The prostitute replied, "I said, I am not a man". Jerome replied, "You see little brother, how his Adams' apple moved, while he is talking. Also, he has very big hands. Fungi hurry up and roll your window back up because this is a man". Fungi replied, "Oh, shit! You are right, let's get out of here".

Fungi rolled his window up and put his car in overdrive. He speeded a hundred, on the R.P.M/Revolutions per mileage on the dashboard inside his car. When Fungi finally reached the destination of his brother's house, Anthony waited in the back seat. Fungi and Jerome walked to the front door and knocked. A woman opened the door to allow Fungi and Jerome to enter.

CHAPTER 5
REUNITE STATE SIDE DRUG DEALER

Anthony waited patiently inside the car. Daylight began to break so; he decided to take a quick nap, before they return to get him. When Anthony woke up, it was clear. It was late morning. Fungi and Jerome decided to walk back to the car. They started arguing, and Fungi became terribly sad. The woman who had opened the door, reported the brother of Fungi, had died of a drug overdose during the early night. The woman was the wife of Fungi's brother. The brother's body was placed in a Maryland hospital.

Fungi was upset with Jerome. Fungi thought, Jerome delayed his trip by mingling with the prostitute. Fungi promised his brother, he would not stray from traveling directly to his house. Now, Fungi would not ever get to speak to his brother alive again. Fungi replied, "Anthony, I am leaving you responsible for my car so; you, all can make it back home to North Carolina. I don't trust your brother anymore; and I must stay for a while to help my brother's wife".

Fungi departed with his brother's wife to the hospital. Before Fungi left, Anthony replied, "Fungi, you don't have to worry. I will make sure; your car gets home safely. We all will pray; God will be with you through your endeavors. Peace and God be with you. Anthony got in the driver's seat of Fungi's car, while Jerome was in the passenger's seat. Then, he drove away as Fungi waved goodbye in another vehicle.

Jerome confirmed; he was tired of being friends with Fungi. He felt, as if he was doing Fungi a favor. Then, Fungi tries to put the blame on him because he didn't get a chance to spend time with his brother, before his death. This was Jerome's last time; he would show remorse to Fungi for any situation. Jerome replied, "From this minute until the end of days, you and Fungi can be friends. I resign my friendship with Fungi".

Anthony replied, "Well tell Fungi, I must do another military assignment in Georgia. When I make my return, we can get together again". Anthony hoped by the time, he returned to Winston-Salem, NC, Jerome and Fungi would have made up their differences. He enjoyed being around his brother and Fungi. Although, if a serious conflict occurred between those two, he probably would have to quit dealing with Fungi.

Anthony drove to his assignment in Georgia. Where he was station, it was at Ft Benning, Ga and home of the Infantry. There he decided; he was going to live a clean life from drugs, settle down and get married. Maybe, he would have children and retire in the military, right at this location. The life in Georgia was hospitable. Anthony did meet his future wife in the Ft Benning, Ga area and eventually married her at a young age.

Anthony lived drug free for a short time. Then, one day his wife Pricilla found a distant cousin, who recently had moved in the area. The cousin was a lady, who was married to a military man. The cousin's name was Angela, and her husband's name was Tyrone. Angela had a similar personality as Pricilla. They were both kind and simple to please. Tyrone on the other hand was different. He was experienced, living in a variety of locations. In return, it made him more cautious and difficult to please.

Tyrone was considered a big guy by Anthony's observation. His size was 6 foot 2 inches; and he weighed 250 pounds. When Tyrone spoke, his voice was loud; and sometimes, he would stutter. Although, this was not a signed of insecurity. Tyrone was always confident and carried himself with style. There were times, when his thinking was a little unorthodox but; he was efficient enough to know, how to explain his position in a debate. Tyrone figured; if you can't beat them then, talk real kindly to them because he enjoyed being friendly.

One day, Anthony's wife Pricilla invited her cousins to a cookout. Tyrone immediately began to persuade Anthony into drinking alcohol and smoking marijuana. In the beginning, Anthony refused but; Tyrone insisted. Tyrone replied, "This is how family members operated. Every family member either drinks, smoked or did both. We enjoy getting high down here in the south". Anthony was skeptical because he was new to the family and was trying to quit.

Anthony tried hard to adjust to Pricilla's cousins. As he got acquainted to Pricilla's cousins, he realized all the celebrating with the drugs and alcohol overwhelmed him. Anthony can't be quiet anymore. He came out his shyness to prove to Tyrone; he could drink with the best of them. Anthony showed Tyrone, North Carolina people knows how to celebrate also. He began to talk and drink more to fit in with Pricilla's family.

Tyrone enjoyed Anthony's kindness greatly. He influenced Anthony to drink more. Then, Anthony got intoxicated and could not control his actions. Tyrone felt comfortable with Anthony and drove him to a drug house. While Anthony waited inside Tyrone's vehicle, Tyrone bought cocaine from the drug house. Tyrone offered cocaine to Anthony but, Anthony informed him; he smoked only marijuana instead of sniffing cocaine. Tyrone felt; he was obligated to persuade Anthony, to try cocaine.

On that day, Anthony remembers drinking alcohol, smoking marijuana and sniffing cocaine. Anthony knows; he drank a lot of Hennessey liquor, took a couple puffs of marijuana and woke up tasting cocaine in his mouth. He was so high; he couldn't recall, how he made it at home. The next day, Tyrone replied, "If anyone tells, what we were doing then, I am coming after them. I believe, you shouldn't even tell your wife, what we did". Anthony replied, "You can trust me, I am not telling no one".

On another occasion, Pricilla invited her cousins to Anthony's party gathering. Pricilla noticed; Tyrone and Anthony were drinking a lot together again. Anthony did not know Pricilla was a big drinker. He never knew, Pricilla enjoyed drinking alcohol or using street drugs. Suddenly, Pricilla interrupts Anthony and Tyrone's conversation while informs them; she enjoys getting high. Anthony was shocked. Pricilla grabs a beer. She replied, "If anybody have some marijuana, include me in because I need to smoke some marijuana".

Anthony was stunned and confused at his wife's statement. He was trying to deviate from during drugs. Anthony was only doing drugs to blend with Pricilla's family. Since now, he finds out his wife enjoys using street drugs too. Soon, Anthony begins to believe; he is doomed to be a drug addict. He figured; No reason in pretending, not to enjoy drugs anymore. It is time to get familiar with the neighborhood street drug dealers because everyone here loves to use drugs.

When Anthony started thinking about drugs, it reminded him about Fungi. Anthony decides to call his brother Jerome and explain, how he needs connections to street drugs because it is what his wife enjoys. Jerome replied, "Well, whenever you are in town, try to contact Fungi. Fungi is big time now, ever since his brother passed away. After Anthony finished talking to Jerome, he gave Fungi a phone call. Fungi was terribly upset with Anthony because Anthony didn't notify him personally; he had moved to Georgia.

Anthony gave Fungi a personal apology and notify him; his life was in disarray. It was over a year; and Anthony was married. He had not visited his mother, since his marriage or heard from Fungi. Anthony was previously afraid to inform Fungi of his address because he figured; he would be shipped somewhere else unexpectedly. Fungi accepted his apology and gave him an invitation to call him for whenever he steps in North Carolina again.

The next time, Anthony traveled to his hometown, life was different in Winston-Salem, NC. The drugs on the street had run rapidly. Fungi had a stronghold on the areas drug market. When Fungi's brother passed away, it caused him to step in his brother's footsteps. The first phone call Anthony made to Fungi for drugs, Fungi assumed they would be able to spend time together. Anthony informed Fungi; he was a married man and had to conduct himself as a married man.

Anthony was married and had a daughter on the way. He notified Fungi; he was a family man now. Fungi replied, "I respect you being a family man. I am not going to give you any problems. I only have to pick up a drug shipment; and I need you to ride with me". Anthony rode with Fungi to get the drugs. They arrived at an establishment, where two guys who were blood brothers, stayed together. The brothers' names were Pistol and Bullet.

Fungi and Anthony entered the house. Pistol replied, "Welcome, come one, come all". Immediately, Anthony notices some guys, sitting on the sofa and sniffing cocaine. Pistol is holding a handgun straight up in his hand. Pistol informs Fungi; cocaine was on the table for anybody to enjoy. Fungi replied, "Thanks, maybe later". Pistol replied, "Let us take a little walk". Then, Fungi, Anthony and Pistol walked down to the kitchen, through the hallway.

While they were walking, evidence of more people was heard on the way to the kitchen. Anthony and Fungi noticed; 2 women standing in the hallway. The women were being casual, talking, and drinking with others. Fungi instantly start chatting with a woman, who appeared to be the most sociable. He inquired; you women are here for business or pleasure. The women informed; a little bit of both.

They were there to test and buy new drugs. Fungi replied, "We are here for the same reason.

One woman, who had lighter skin than the other person, looked at Anthony. She asked him, "You are here to smoke drugs". Anthony replied, "No, I am only here with a friend to assist him picking up a package". The woman replied, "You don't appear to be a drug exchange dealer". Anthony replied, "I sell randomly". The woman replied, "I have not come across you before". Anthony replied, "I deal discreetly". The woman was named Ethel; and she spoke to Anthony directly.

Ethel replied, "If you are trying to locate a supplier then, call me at this number. Here is my phone number. You appear to be a gentleman, who I might could work with in a time of need". Fungi touches Anthony on his shoulder to get his attention. Fungi replied, "Nice looking women but; I know, you are happily married. Please Anthony, we must focus on business and not pleasure. We must keep our focus on Pistol and Bullet". Pistol replied, "I believe, my older brother is ready to see you guys now".

Once they arrived in the kitchen, a group of people were playing cards on a kitchen table. Pistol alerted Bullet; Fungi was here with a friend behind you because Bullet was playing cards. Bullet replied, "Hello Fungi, what have you got for me today". Fungi pulls out this brown paper bag, out his cargo shirt pocket. Inside the bag, there was a huge chunk of marijuana, stuffed in a plastic bag.

Fungi gave the plastic bag to Bullet. He had a smaller plastic bag also. Fungi replied, "That's right! Anthony, I have here is a gift for you. Thanks, for riding along with me". Fungi gave Anthony the smaller plastic bag. Anthony peeped at the smaller plastic bag and was grateful to be given a gift. Bullet reached on the table, where he had a stack of money located and grabbed a stash of money. He gave it to Fungi. Then, Bullet replied, "Don't go just yet. I want you to try some cocaine".

Bullet passed Fungi a glass pipe with crystal methane cocaine inside the pipe. Fungi replied, "What's this?" Bullet replied, "The new drug on the street called crack". Fungi takes a puff and pass it to Anthony. Anthony takes a puff and instantly feels the stimulation from the drug. Then, Bullet rolls a marijuana cigar, takes a puff and pass it to Fungi. Fungi takes a puff and pass it to Anthony. Anthony begins to feel, as if he is floating in the air.

Anthony starts feeling a nice high from the drugs. He begins to feel comfortable. The state of being cautious, slips his mind and he allows his guard to go down. Anthony decides to uncover his jacket and take a seat in the kitchen. He begins to have a craving to relax. Out of nowhere, a guy runs out the kitchen door and pass him. Bullet stops laughing and calls Pistol's name. Bullet replied, "Pistol go get him, now!" Pistol takes off running behind him through the kitchen door.

Bullet informs everybody to get out the house. Fungi and Anthony exits out the kitchen door with everyone else, as Bullet is the last one to leave. Pistol meets up with the guy out back and tackles him. Then, he begins to pistol whip the guy, while he was fussing with the man. The guy tries to respond to Bullet, as he appeared. No words could be understood from the guy because too much blood, was coming from his mouth. In addition, little crystal rocks of cocaine were spitting up, out from his mouth.

Pistol held his handgun to the guy's temple of his forehead, while keeping him face down in the ground. Pistol replied, "Don't you ever steal from us again! I bet not ever see you around here because I will break both your legs, for running away from me". Bullet turned around to observe the audience looking. Bullet looked towards Pistol. Bullet replied to Pistol, "Okay, little brother! Everything is going to be okay. We don't want to make too much of a scene. This what happens sometimes. It could have been worse".

Pistol allowed the guy to leave on foot going the opposite direction, away from the house. Everyone else departed towards some other direction. Bullet replied, "Next time somebody steals, kill them because he messed up my good time". Anthony looked at Fungi with wide eyes. He replied to Fungi, "You sure, you want to do business with these brothers". Pistol and Bullet walked back to their house. Fungi followed behind them.

Fungi informed Bullet; if all parties are satisfied, he and Anthony will be leaving now. Bullet retrieved a brown paper bag to give to Fungi so; Fungi could carry his money without being noticed. Inside the brown bag, Bullet gave Fungi some crystal meth cocaine as a hospitality gift. Then, Fungi returned Anthony to his mom's house. After Anthony arrived at his mom's house, Fungi replied, "Thanks for being my partner. Anthony, you can have the crack cocaine; in addition to the marijuana, I gave you".

Anthony was shocked. He now, had a bag of marijuana and a drug called crack. Fungi insisted; Anthony accepted all the drugs he received. Fungi replied, "Don't be shy. Drugs is drugs, they all do something to you. Personally, I don't want any more temptation to do drugs. I only want to sell marijuana. That's all, I am doing. I am not trying to get hooked on crack. I don't want to be selling marijuana and sniffing crack".

Anthony replied, "Stay well partner. Be careful, if you deal with them guys, Pistol and Bullet. They meant business for real. Now, I have my drugs and a drug connection. It is time for me to return to Georgia with my wife. Fungi, you take care. I will see you again soon". Before Anthony decided to leave home, he called the woman named Ethel. Anthony wanted to know exactly, what kind of operation, she was running. When Anthony conveyed with Ethel over the phone, Ethel informed him; she wanted to see him again.

Ethel lived in a government assistance apartment. Her mom and her grown adult daughter lived there also. Ethel's grown adult daughter had a child, who lived with them too. Ethel sold drugs, out of her apartment. She had government assistance clients, who bought drugs from her and was dependent on the drugs to get high. Ethel kept measurement scales to measure the drugs and plastic bags for storing the drugs, inside her apartment. She hired neighborhood people to assist with delivering the drugs to customers.

Ethel's operation fascinated Anthony because she was successful, operating a business in her home. She informed Anthony; her mother sold drugs to make a living, and her grandmother did the same thing also. Ethel replied, "Now, my daughter wants to get involved because she finds, I am successful". Ethel's entire family, from grandmother to daughter, had been living on government assistance and drug money. Anthony wondered about Ethel; did she ever fantasized about having a different life.

Before Anthony could ask Ethel about living a different life; and having a life without drugs, Ethel proudly began to speak. Ethel replied, "I have visited other lifestyles but; here is what makes me happy. I could never leave my family because they might believe; I think, I am more important than them". Anthony began to have sympathy, for Ethel's belief. While Anthony was there visiting Ethel, he taught her, there was more to selling drugs. Ethel was good at selling anything and making friends so; Anthony introduced her to an on-line business.

With an on-line business, Ethel began selling store products from home and studying education to receive her high school degree. Although, Ethel's mother became jealous of the idea. Ethel's mother decided to make threats to move in with a drug dealer unless, Ethel decided to quit her business and education. Unfortunately, Anthony found out; Ethel's mother had a relationship with Bullet. With Anthony's advice, Ethel's mother gained confidence to leave Bullet and the drugs alone. In the process, Bullet abused Ethel's mother; and she ended up in the hospital.

Then, Anthony returned to Georgia for military duty. Work was as normal. Pricilla's attitude appeared to change daily. Anthony thought; Pricilla was a mellow person but apparently, it was not the case. Pricilla felt the need to have more income in the home. She passed a childcare class and started advertising for business. Anthony believed; she felt a need to buy drugs for relaxation and stress. Pricilla enjoyed the feeling and excitement, which occurred around drugs.

While Pricilla started her own daycare business to earn extra money for her home. At night, she would relax after daycare by getting high to relieve the stress. When company arrived, Pricilla entertained with drugs for excitement. Anthony would allow her to get high a little because he wanted peace in the home. He politely introduced the drugs, Fungi gave to him and issued it to Pricilla.

It didn't take very long, before Pricilla started craving for the drugs nightly. Pricilla enjoyed the drugs so much; she got addicted to the drugs. Anthony began to realize; he made a big mistake. There was no way, he could support this kind of habit on his family's income. To prevent a financial problem, Anthony decided to pick up an additional job, working at Domino's Pizza delivery shop. He became stressed so; in the process, he started to do drugs.

Anthony lived too far away from his friend Fungi to make any drug deals in North Carolina. He had no choice but to confide in Pricilla's cousin Tyrone, for a request of a quick fix of drugs. Tyrone would sell drugs to Anthony. In the process, they grew to become good friends. Tyrone would invite Anthony over to his house to watch the football games at drink gatherings or secrete rendezvous. Most of the secrete rendezvous would consist of Tyrone cheating on his wife, buying drugs, and other bad deeds.

Tyrone was a womanizer. He enjoyed flirting with other women besides his wife, every chance he got. One day, him and Anthony ended up over a lady's house to buy marijuana. While Anthony waited inside the vehicle, Tyrone was occupied in the lady's house for over an hour. Tyrone walked out the lady's house, fixing his clothes on his body with the marijuana in his pocket. He had a disappointing expression on his face.

Anthony observed Tyrone. Tyrone was so disappointed and Anthony, didn't know why because Tyrone had the marijuana in his pocket. Tears was running down Tyrone's face. Anthony replied, "Is everything okay?" Tyrone replied, "I love my wife but; I don't deserve her. I need to do better but; I can't help it. The drugs keep talking to me". Anthony replied, "What are they saying?" Tyrone replied, "Get your kitty, kitty! Go get your kitty, kitty".

Anthony replied, "It's the chronic talking to you. The drugs are influencing you. The rap music, you are listening to also. Try to keep your mind focus. Don't do too much talking, when you are handling business. It is easy to mix business with personal feelings. You should stay out of trouble this way". Anthony didn't want to believe; Tyrone had a drug problem because he enjoyed socializing with Tyrone. He hoped Tyrone would eventually figure out all his disfunctions, he had personally.

CHAPTER 6
MEETING WITH 2 DRUG DEALERS

Tyrone was a Captain in the Army; and Anthony was a Sergeant in the Army. Although, in regular life, they were just ordinary friends. Anthony bought drugs from Tyrone, which provided drugs for his wife; and he worked two jobs. Anthony was employed at Domino's Pizza, as a pizza delivery person. During this time, a phone call from an office warehouse had ordered a lot of pizzas. Anthony excepted the order and delivered the pizzas. He figured; he would receive a big tip for delivering the pizzas. In addition, Anthony was low on drugs and needed to make extra money on tips.

When Anthony arrived at the office warehouse with the pizzas, someone allowed him to enter an office room, where there was an office desk and a computer on top. Hanging up and showing was a petition made up of curtains, which open wide. The curtains led you to a big empty space room. A man came through the curtains. Anthony could hear something happening on the other side of the curtains. He also smelled marijuana smoke. Then, he heard talking and clapping behind the curtains.

It sounded familiar, as if a play was being conducted. A man dressed in tight pants with a tight-fitting shirt, greeted Anthony. He was short but muscular. The man replied, "You can put the pizza down beside the computer, Sir". Anthony replied, "Alright, your total is ninety dollars for all the pizza". The man replied, "You look very fit. I bet you have served in the military?" Anthony replied, "Yes! I am serving in the military, now. I do pizza delivery, part time". The man replied, "That's patriotic of you. Thanks!"

The man replied, "I bet you know how to dance good?" Anthony replied, "Dance! I guess, I can do okay". Then, a lady in a two-piece bathing suit, poked her head out through the curtain. The lady was extremely good-looking. She replied, "Where is the pizza? I am hungry". The lady glanced her eyes at Anthony and winked at him. Then, she waved her hand. Anthony politely waved back. The curtain cracked open wider. Anthony witnessed more people in skimpy clothes and dancing to music.

In a big open bay area, there was a stage with a decoration display of dancers, cut-out cardboard displays, and music for visitors. The man replied, "Woman! I will announce when I have the pizza, after I pay for it". The woman replied, "Okay, I was just asking". She pulled the curtain back shut again; and the music stopped. The man replied, "Hey, pizza man. If possible, can you dance for me?" Anthony looked at him. He replied, "No, I don't think so". The man shook his head. He replied, "Oh, okay. Let me write you a check".

The man calls the lady to return through the curtain. The man replied, "I want to introduce you to my assistant named Candice, who is known as the candy stripper". The lady peeped through the curtains and smiled, while smoking a marijuana cigarette. The man replied, "If you will believe, I run a strip club. Do you like her? If you do then, you can see her perform here tonight at the Amateur Strip Rally. I can get you, V.I.P seats for an exchange of a discount of the pizzas".

Anthony thinks a minute. He replied, "Okay, you give me two tickets to the Amateur Strip Rally. In addition, a bag of marijuana because what she is smoking smells good. I will subtract twenty dollars, off the price of the pizzas". The lady gave a big smile. The man replied, "You got yourself a deal. Now, Candice go grab the pizzas because my employees are hungry". Anthony received the check for the pizzas with two tickets and a bag of marijuana from the man. He was left feeling, as if he had made a good deal for the marijuana.

Afterwards, Anthony decided to make a phone call to Fungi. Fungi answered the phone and informed Anthony; the drug business is booming. He was doing extremely well with exchanging drugs for money. Fungi offers Anthony an assistant job, if he ever decided to leave the military. Fungi replied, "I love my life. I have my own network. Furthermore, I smoke my own stuff; and sell it when, I want to. Frequently, women flock to have sex with me. As for my friends, my business is always open for new partners".

Anthony replied, "Fungi, I appreciate the offer. I have much love for you, just as a brother. Although, I am not trying to be caught up in selling drugs. When, I come home, my support is always for you and your endeavors". Fungi replied, "If whenever you decide to move back this way, I will make sure everything is straight in your life. Your family, income, hobbies and whatever; I will take care of it. You, me and including your brother are family for life". Anthony was surprised. Fungi included his brother but; he was relieved and overjoyed.

On one occasion, while in Georgia, Anthony meets his Aunt on his wife's side of the family. Her named was Aunt Ester. Then, after Anthony meets Aunt Ester, he is introduced to Aunt Ester husband. His name was Uncle Earl. Aunt Ester and Uncle Earl are both heavy drinkers. Pricilla had recently delivered her second child. The baby was born premature with birth disabilities. The baby became physically and mentally slow developed. While Pricilla's Aunt and Uncle were drinking alcoholic beverages, Pricilla decided to introduce her family and the newborn baby.

Uncle Earl viewed the baby. He replied, "This baby is so small. I think, I will name it Half Pint. Your oldest daughter, I will call her

Funtasia because she is funny. Peradventure because of circumstances, the daughter's nicknames stuck with Pricilla's entire relatives. Uncle Earl enjoyed drinking so much; he carried and drank alcohol wherever he ventured. Anthony met up with Uncle Earl at the city park. He brought along, his recently adopted puppy.

Anthony named his adopted puppy Kilo because the puppy was worth 1000 dollars to Anthony. He figured; it would be nice to take the puppy and his children to the park. Then, Anthony could allow Uncle Earl to become acquainted with the puppy and his children. When Anthony arrived at the park, there were park rangers mingling in the parking lot in front of the park. Anthony noticed; Uncle Earl was conversating with a park ranger. As Anthony parked beside Uncle Earl, he greeted him.

Uncle Earl replied, "Hello, nephew. Who, do you have there with you?" Anthony replied, "I have Funtasia. Also, I have Half Pint and Kilo. We are about to have a lovely time, here in the park. My new addition to my family, Kilo is a little shy but; you can tell it is mix with something. Hey, Uncle Earl come closer to get a better look!" As the park ranger overheard Anthony talking, he immediately became cautious. The park ranger replied, "Yes, Sir! I think, I will walk with you and your nephew to his automobile also".

The park ranger and Uncle Earl began walking towards Anthony's automobile. The park ranger grabbed his handheld radio; as if he was going to make an announcement or something to some other park rangers. Anthony presumed everything was fine. When Uncle Earl and the park ranger appeared close enough to observe what was in Anthony's automobile, Anthony opened the door. The park ranger quickly jumped in front of Uncle Earl. Anthony was fine with the park ranger looking in his vehicle. He didn't know, this was causing any trouble.

The park rangers were on high alert with Uncle Earl. Uncle Earl had been cited numerous times from the park rangers for drinking in the park. This park ranger was warning Uncle Earl, this would be his last occurrence, if caught again in the park using alcohol or illegal drugs. Unfortunately, Anthony had no knowledge, he was putting Uncle Earl in a bad situation with the park ranger. The park ranger figured; Uncle Earl knows better. This time, I will catch him red handed with someone doing drugs. I am going to lock him up for good.

Anthony got out his vehicle and closed the door. He replied, "Park ranger is everything okay because my puppy Kilo, don't have a lease on. I would hate for my puppy to escape outside because he is a trouble to fetch". The park ranger looked at Anthony. Then, he looked at Uncle Earl. The park ranger replied, "I am just making sure, you don't have no alcohol or illegal drugs in the vehicle". Anthony looked at Uncle Earl. He replied, "Why would you think, I would be having something illegal?"

The park ranger replied, "Ask your Uncle". He departed with a greeting to Anthony's children, while patting the puppy on his head and left. Uncle Earl politely replied, "Hello" to Funtasia and Half Pint". Then, he commented the puppy was beautiful. The park ranger informed all the other park rangers; the park was cleared of all park violations. Anthony, his kids, Uncle Earl, and the puppy were the only people left in the State park. Anthony informed Uncle Earl; peradventure they need to create some other type of nicknames for his daughters because their nicknames draw attention.

Uncle Earl appeared to be offended. He replied, "You don't have to associate with me, if I embarrass you too much. I am not going to the parks anymore to have fun". Anthony tried to make up to Uncle Earl for offending him. He volunteered and bought alcohol at the liquor store, as a peace offering. Uncle Earl replied, "Anthony, what is your favorite liquor?" Anthony replied, "Whisky". Anthony walked-in the liquor store and bought a half-gallon of Whisky for Uncle Earl and him. Then, shortly following, Uncle Earl walked-in the liquor store and bought a half-gallon of Vodka.

Uncle Earl replied, "I am sorry but, I don't like to drink Whisky. I am a Vodka drinker. Now, you have your liquor; and I have mines". As everybody arrived at Uncle Earl's apartment, Anthony's children rushed inside to be greeted by Aunt Ester. Anthony tied the puppy to a tree. Uncle Earl and he spent time outside with the puppy. Uncle Earl had hand carried the Whisky and Vodka to the tree. He sat it down on the ground. Uncle Earl replied, "Here's your liquor. When you open it, throw away the bottle cap because you don't need it anymore".

Anthony was confused. He thought; I know, Uncle Earl just told me, he doesn't like drinking Whisky. If I throw away the bottle cap, us together must be going to drink the Whisky. Anthony threw away his Whisky bottle cap, thinking Uncle Earl had suddenly changed his mind. Uncle Earl grabbed his Vodka, twisted the bottle cap off, and threw it away. Anthony could not believe his eyes. Now, they had to drink, 2 half-gallon liquor bottles because they had no caps for either liquor bottle. Anthony replied, "Uncle Earl have you gone crazy! Who is going to drink, all this liquor?"

CHAPTER 7
THE DRUG LIFE

Anthony began searching for the liquor bottle caps, just in case, they wanted to save some of the liquor. Uncle Earl put the Vodka of liquor up to his mouth and drunk about half of the liquor in one gulp. Anthony was shocked and stopped instantly looking for the liquor bottle caps. He found some garden chairs for Uncle Earl and himself. Then, he took a seat in one of the chairs and enjoyed Uncle Earl putting on a show. Uncle Earl replied, "You don't have to worry. The children and you will stay with us all night". Anthony thought; no way. Who is going to be drinking, while up all night? Anthony thought; this is going to be a rough night.

It turned out, Anthony did stay all night and part of an early morning with Uncle Earl. They consumed liquor all night until Uncle Earl completed his bottle of Vodka; and Anthony was intoxicated. The children were in good hands with Uncle Ester but, they never had seen their father intoxicated as this. The children and Anthony arrived at their home the next day. Pricilla was very upset. The next day, Anthony spent time with her so, she could get high and make up for time lost. Anthony realized; getting high everyday wasn't easy. He tried to give up alcohol and drugs again.

With Pricilla's toxic family members, staying sober was almost impossible. Anthony realized; he was going to have to do something drastic to stay sober every day. Pricilla was becoming addictive to drugs and including himself also. The final straw was when Anthony had to work all day. Anthony was working two jobs, the Army and delivering pizzas. It was Pricilla's birthday. Anthony had notified her; he would do something nice for her the next day. Although, it didn't matter because Pricilla was furious.

This was the first time; Anthony was not able to spend time with his wife on her birthday. Pricilla request was she wanted to have a birthday party in her home without depending on Anthony's presence. Anthony notified her; he didn't feel comfortable allowing her to have a birthday party without him being there. In perspective, he did not trust a whole lot of people celebrating in his home, while he was at work. During certain days, Anthony was able to leave ahead of schedule because there was a death threat at the pizza place job. An unruly customer, who Anthony serviced before, complained he was robbed of his drugs.

Later, Anthony found out his co-worker rob the guy because of a story; he told about receiving marijuana from a stripper's club. The guy promised; he would get his revenge on the pizza place by doing a drive-by shooting. Anthony departed the pizza place early in the night, while the owner stayed for security reasons. While he was traveling home, a stop was made halfway between work and home. Anthony stopped at a local store. He only had 5 minutes travel time left, before making it home. At the store, a person who resided in Anthony's community was there.

The guy who resided in Anthony's community replied, "You are in uniform so; you must still be working". Anthony replied, "No!" The guy replied, "Great! I want to invite you to a house, not too far away. They are having a party. I am on foot. If possible, can you give me a lift?" Anthony replied, "No problem, you know; I stay in the neighborhood also". The guy hopped in Anthony's vehicle and proceeded to direct Anthony, on how to arrive at this party. Pretty soon, the guy instructed Anthony to make a right turn and down the road where he resides.

Anthony replied, "Wait a second. How much further, do we have to go, before we reach this party?" The guy replied, "Only a couple more houses down". Anthony was shocked. He replied, "I apologize but, this party has ended. The guy replied, "Wait a minute, what are you talking about, this party has ended. There is a lot of cars down there". Anthony replied, "At this party, this is my house, where I live. This party is about to be officially cancelled. Furthermore, your ride has ended with me".

Sadly, the guy gets out the vehicle and leave in the opposite direction. Anthony enters his home. He could not believe his eyes. Cousin Tyrone, cousin Angela, Uncle Earl, and Aunt Ester were among Pricilla's guest at her birthday gathering. Then, Pricilla had friends from her daycare clients. They were all drinking, smoking, and having a good time. There was fancy liquor, imported beer, and illegal drugs. All were at the party. Anthony became very irate; he sent everyone home. He noticed everyone was there, except his wife Pricilla.

Anthony began searching for Pricilla. He found her passed out in bed with a beer in her hand. Drugs and alcohol were located all over the place. From then, Anthony made it known; a change of operation needs to occur for his family because they could not function on narcotics. Anthony requested for a change of assignment at his duty station and his family to relocate to North Carolina. As his request for change of assignment became approved, harsh resentment was sent from his wife. Pricilla did not like the idea. Her relatives were disappointed.

In the process, Anthony made special consideration for his family to spend more time with his in-laws, before they moved. Cousin

Tyrone and Angela invited Anthony's family to a cookout. Cousin Tyrone made one last pitch, why they shouldn't move. Uncle Earl and Aunt Ester was at the cookout also. They gave their final goodbyes. Pricilla, the children, and even Kilo the puppy appeared very sad to be leaving. Anthony packed his family in their vehicle and hauled everything they owned to Ft. Bragg, NC military base.

Once Anthony arrived at the military base and became situated with the area, he notified his mother in Winston-Salem, NC. He was now, a permanent resident in the North Carolina area again. Anthony was only about a 2-hour drive from his mom's house. He alerted Tyrone and Angela of his family's address because they might want to come and visit them sometimes. All were fine at their new location in the beginning. Pricilla even turned back to her old self, who Anthony first met. Anthony also changed his habits and became a sober person again.

Life for Anthony's family was simple and normal until boredom set in. Then, Anthony's family decided to make a 2-hour drive and visit Anthony's mother. As Anthony departed Ft. Bragg, he traveled through Fayetteville and finally made it to their destination in Winston-Salem. The city of Winston Salem appeared different than before. The crime in Winston-Salem was twice as bad. Anthony and his family cross over the Winston-Salem borderline. There was North Carolina State Troopers position on the highway for a city roadblock.

Anthony got stopped by State Patrol Troopers for unknown reasons. A Patrol Officer replied, "Good evening Sir. We are doing a routine safety check". Anthony replied, "Safety check for what reasons". The Patrol Officer replied, "I am checking to make sure no one is driving under the influence and have illegal drugs in their vehicle". Please, I need to see your driver's license and registration card". Anthony could tell Pricilla was becoming a little irritate by the delay.

The Patrol Officer noticed; Anthony was wearing a military uniform on his driver's license. He replied, "Thank you, for your time and service with the military. You can continue with your trip". Anthony and his family were relieved to be finally moving again. They continued down the highway but, they passed through another roadblock. Anthony wondered; what is happening in his city. He decided to by-pass the roadblock and turned off the highway. Then, Anthony arrived shortly in the downtown area.

In the downtown area of Winston-Salem, Anthony observed some drug addicts socializing up and down the sidewalks. Right in plain view, city people were smoking dope, buying and selling dope. At one point, Anthony stops at the traffic light and someone tries to sell him drugs. Anthony politely replied, "No thanks. I don't do drugs anymore". The drug dealer replied, "What about the pretty lady? I got some white horse. You know called smack, the good stuff". Anthony replied, "I told you, we don't do drugs".

Anthony decided to speed away through the traffic light. When he arrived at his mother's house, he realized things have changed there also. All Anthony's acquaintances, in his mom's neighborhood, were either dead or on drugs. Fortunately, Anthony's brother had moved away from home. This caused Anthony's mother to be alone in her house. Anthony became concerned about the drug use around the area. Peradventure, it would not be a problem but; Anthony's longtime friend recognized his arrival over his mom's house.

Anthony's friend decided to visit him over his mom's house. The doorbell rings at Anthony's mom's house. Anthony's mom answers the door and was greeted by Anthony's friend. Anthony's friend is drunk and high on drugs. Anthony's friend replied, "Hello, Ms. Jackson. It has been a long time since we have mingled". Anthony's mother replied, "We have never mingled. You must be talking about my son. I don't mingle with people, the age of my children". Anthony eavesdrops on the conversation.

Then, Anthony looked at his friend and could tell, he was intoxicated. Anthony decided to advise his friend to leave because he is delusional. His friend replied, "Wait, I want to ask you for some money". Anthony replied, "I don't have any money; and you must go". Anthony's friend replied, "Who wants me to go? Why, I have to leave?" Anthony replied, "It is best, you go because I said so; or I will kick you, out the door". Anthony begins to make a direct charge at his friend in an aggressive manner. So happened, the friend decides to run out the door before Anthony could have an encounter with him.

Now, Anthony is a little concerned about his mother's safety. Anthony informs his mother; his military time left, is his last days, of his military career. He has decided to leave the military for good and make his home in Winston-Salem. Anthony wants to be close to his mother. He believes; his mother is not safe being alone. Then, his mother notifies Jerome; Anthony has returned home. The next day, Jerome has phone called to notify Fungi; Anthony has relocated back home. Help is needed from Fungi because Anthony will be requiring a job.

Fungi calls Anthony on his cell phone. Anthony answers his phone. Then, Fungi replied, "Hello Anthony! I know, you probably could use a job. I have information to help you". When Anthony was finally released from the military, he saved money and bought a new home in the area. Anthony had obtained a job but gathered information from Fungi on additional employment. He notified Fungi; I do not want to be involved with any drugs anymore. Fungi informed; he understood this. He knew, Anthony didn't feel comfortable in dangerous situation and probably preferred a job, where you don't have to be supervised.

Fungi replied, "I have 2 associates, who work for a business. They make money on commission working alone, and no time clock". Anthony replied, "This is the part-time job, I need". When Anthony reported for work at the new part-time job, he reported to Fungi's associates. Bullet and Pistol, who were Fungi's associates, also were drug dealers. They looked familiar to Anthony but; during this time, things appeared fuzzy. He couldn't place where; he had met them. Pistol replied, "My brother and I, make a lot of money selling meats for a company named Nebraska Meats".

Anthony arrived for the briefing with Nebraska Meats. Soon afterwards, he could begin selling meats immediately. Nebraska Meats informed Anthony; their meat-selling business is one of the most rewarding companies in the world. If a person sold a complete package of meats: which consist of seafood, pork, and beef then, a 1000 dollars profit could be made. Anthony figured; this is better than selling drugs. If the profit is this good, who needs to sell drugs.

The Nebraska Meat company informed; each new person is on a trial-based program. The new people would have to be trained by a trusted employee. The company emphasized new employees to pay close attention to their trainers because they are experienced sellers with the company. Nebraska Meats placed Anthony with Pistol because they lived in the same area. Pistol instantly notified Anthony; to listen to him and do not open his mouth. He kept stressing for Anthony to watch and learn, how to sell.

Pistol had a red Camaro car. He drove the car with boxes of meat stored in his trunk. Anthony was wondering, if the meat would spoil inside his trunk. He decided to ask Pistol about the meat. Pistol replied, "What did, I tell you. Shut up and don't ask any questions until I tell you too. You don't know anything about this business. I will tell you now, the meat doesn't have time to spoil because I sell it quickly. I sell my meat in one day. What all, I don't sell, I buy for my family. That is why, it is so important to sell. My family does not need all this meat".

Pistol informed Anthony; the first stop, where we sell meat, is in Greensboro. A stop was made at a residence in Greensboro. Pistol replied, "New guy wait here in the automobile". Anthony observed Pistol knocking on a residence door and shouting "Nebraska Meats". No one came to the door. Pistol returned to the Camaro. He opened his glove compartment and withdrew a handgun. Anthony replied,

"Hey, what is going on?" Pistol replied, "New guy scream my name if someone comes out this front door".

Pistol marched to the back door of the residence. Anthony replied, "Hey Pistol. I thought; we were selling meats. Now, what are we doing? I am not here for any trouble". Pistol replied, "We are here to sell meat". A guy peeps out the window of a residence and then, opens his front door. Pistol replied, "That's right Sir! We are meat sellers". A guy comes out the front door. Pistol hits him upside the head with his handgun. The guy falls out on the ground. Pistol informed; where is my money, you owe me?

The guy replied, "I have your money, right here". Pistol replied, "This better be all of it". The guy replied, "I will give you, the rest of it soon, I promise you". Pistol replied, "Give me, your dope as a replacement". The guy gives Pistol, a bag of marijuana. Pistol replied, "Alright, we even now. If I come back, this way again, I don't want no problems". The guy replied, "It's okay with me". Pistol notified Anthony; we are leaving now. Pistol and Anthony departed. Anthony replied, "Hey, Pistol. I am not going to be out here robbing people. I don't need money this bad".

Pistol informed Anthony; the guy owed him money. He was tired of listening to him talk. Pistol replied, "Look, you are a new guy. If you want to learn, how to sell meat then, shut up and stop talking. This is the first step to learning because I can tell, you are not cut out for this type of work. Before we go any farther up the road, I can return, you back to the company. By the way, have you ever sold anything before?" Anthony replied, "Yes, I was a pizza delivery salesman". Pistol replied, "This doesn't count because this is mostly indoor sales".

Pistol informed Anthony; this job consisted of outdoor sales. Sometimes, you must sell in the street, on the corner, or in your automobile. Pistol replied, "Do you even have a sales pitch or either a phrase to get people attention to buy things?" Anthony didn't have a sales pitch or never thought, he needed one. Pistol replied, "I bet, you don't know anything about a sales pitch! You will notice; if you are with me, I teach you all this. Second, note; I shouldn't show, you anything because if you talk, you are going to scare my customers away".

Anthony replied, "Pistol, if you have not noticed, I am here to make money too. I need to learn how to sell". Pistol replied, "I don't care about you or if you make any money! Although, one thing, I do care about! You better keep your mouth closed". Pistol drove to Gibsonville, outside of Greensboro, NC to refill his automobile with gas. Anthony replied, "Why are we going, this direction to sell meats? We should be selling meats in Winston-Salem. All my known contacts to perspective buyers are there, plus my family. I can make a lot of sells there".

Pistol replied, "I don't sell meats in my city because every meat-seller from there, is doing business. See, I am smarter than, the average meat-seller. When I sell, I travel as far away from the company so; I don't bump into any co-workers". Pistol notified Anthony; to stay put in the automobile, as they arrived at the gas station. Then, Pistol paid for the gas, inside the station. Anthony noticed; all kinds of people getting out their vehicles and entering the gas station.

Anthony witnessed an elderly man socializing with a military soldier, who was traveling to Ft. Bragg, NC. He exits the vehicle and walks up to the soldier while informing; I am with a meat company. I am selling meat. The soldier replied, "I eat free, in a dining facility. I don't cook". The elderly man replied, "What kind of meats, do you have Sir?" The military soldier walked away; and Pistol walks out the store. Anthony informs the elderly man to walk to the trunk of the automobile and observe.

Anthony screams out, "USDA grade A plus meats!" The elderly man gets worried because Anthony was making a scene. The elderly man replied, "No, forget it. I changed my mind. Not this time but, maybe another time". Pistol observed the elderly man walking away; and Anthony making a scene. Pistol was upset. Pistol replied, "See, you made a big mistake". Anthony replied, "How you figured, this was my fault". Pistol replied, "I told you to keep your mouth closed. You don't know, what to say, or how to make a deal. You are scaring, the customers away".

Pistol stands on the hood of his car and shouts. He replied, "I got Nebraska Steaks for sale. We got seafood, pork chops and T. Bone steaks all at a low discount". People began walking away. It appeared, as if no one was interested. Pistol whispered to Anthony, in a low voice. He replied, "This is my last time telling you; keep your mouth closed, or I will make you walk back to Winston-Salem. I told you already; I don't care, if you make a sale because I am not trying to feed you". Pistol informed Anthony again; you are scaring the customers away.

Anthony watched the elderly man grabbed his wife's hand, as the elderly man and his wife got inside a vehicle. The elderly couple drove passed a sign on the property which read, "No soliciting to store customers without ownership approval". Anthony observed the sign and found his confidence again to sell. He realized the elderly man could not buy their products because of the no soliciting sign, advertised on the property. During the moment, Anthony informed Pistol; he felt like he could have gotten a sale, if they weren't on store property.

Pistol retrieved an advertisement business card out his bag. He began to read on the card, the company's opening line when someone was interested in buying a product. Then, when a customer wanted to buy the product, a salesperson was supposed to say a closing statement. This is right after the customer purchase the product. Pistol replied, "When making a sale to a customer, this is what, you are supposed to say. That's why; I tell you to keep your mouth shut because you don't know, our valued sales pitch. Until you learn, the company's sales pitch by hard, keep your mouth closed".

Anthony felt he had been deceived. He requested Pistol to allow him to review the business card so, he could get acquainted with the company's sale pitch. Pistol allowed Anthony to review the business card a couple of times. Then, he took it back and put the business card away. Pistol pull out a bag of marijuana, rolled a marijuana cigarette, took a smoke, and gave it to Anthony to smoke. Anthony replied, "No thank you". Then, Pistol made a cell phone call to a friend and drove to his friend's house in a Gibsonville neighborhood, outside of Greensboro.

Once they arrived in the Gibsonville neighborhood, a guy appeared. Pistol gave the guy a marijuana cigarette and smoke it with him. He asked the guy, "If there is someone he knew, who would be interested in buying meats?" The guy replied, "Not now because times are tough. Besides, people's payday was too far away". They were in a predominately Black area but; a Caucasian elderly lady appeared, walking down the street from nowhere. The lady turned and looked at them strangely, while they were in Pistol's car. Pistol looked at the lady and then, the lady walked away.

Pistol replied, "The way I feel, if they wanted me to train then, they should have given me a White boy to train. Two Black guys riding in a Camaro car makes us look, as if we are looking for trouble. It is to unprofessional. I need a White boy to look professional. Now, Anthony became frustrated and irate. Anthony replied, "Now, I have to definitely speak my mind. We are sitting here messing around; and we haven't sold not one box of meats. 3 hours have passed; and half the daylight is over".

Pistol informed, "We could have sold some boxes of meat by now, if you wouldn't have spooked the customers". It was going on twelve, in the afternoon. They still had 5 boxes of meats to sale. Each box had a complete packet of 6 steaks, 2 packs of shrimps, and 6 pork chops with a street value of about 250 dollars. Pistol replied, "We are in Gibsonville, my stumping ground. Next, I will make a last trip to Reidsville, which is about an hour away". After Pistol did not make a sale in Gibsonville, he decided to head on to Reidsville.

As we began traveling to Reidsville, about a half hour away, we stopped in Greensboro. Pistol replied, "New guy, go wait in the car, while I give some money to my baby's mother. Pistol walked in his baby's mother's apartment. While he entered the apartment, a Caucasian woman walked up to Pistol's car. Presently, Anthony was asleep on the passenger side of the vehicle. Anthony's head was by the vehicle door window, as it was cracked. The woman sticks her hand, through the cracked window and rubbed Anthony's head.

Anthony wakes up in the vehicle and finds an attractive Caucasian woman looking down at him, while rubbing his head. She replied, "You are black". Anthony replied, "Yes as far as I know". The Caucasian woman replied, "Pistol, don't like training Black guys. Pistol gets sort of jealous, when a Black guy might become good as him at his trade". Anthony replied, "I am starting to get, the same impression". The Caucasian woman replied, "I hope, you are not married because we can hook up".

Anthony replied, "You must be Pistol's baby's mother". The lady replied, "Yes". Anthony replied, "Look, I am not trying to get in any confrontation with Pistol". The lady replied, "Pistol can't see us. He is in the apartment. I only showed up at Pistol's car because he wanted me to get a box of meat. Pistol is in the apartment with his girlfriend, smoking marijuana and having sex". After Anthony heard this, he became extremely upset. Anthony informed the lady; he will carry the meat back to her apartment; only if he can talk to Pistol.

CHAPTER 8
HOME-STYLE DRUG LIFE

Once Anthony reached the lady's apartment, he found Pistol relaxing on the sofa and smoking dope. Pistol looked at Anthony with disbelief. Pistol replied, "Oh, you found me! I was just about to leave. Thanks for carrying this box of meat for my baby's mother to her apartment. Let's go because time is passing". Anthony peeped at his cell phone. It was 2:00 p.m. Still, they had sold no meat. Pistol and Anthony finally reached their destination in Reidsville, about 30 minutes later.

Pistol replied, "Look new guy, I am high as a kite. I figured; you do understand, this is not working out for us. I am going to try out and see, if you can create some prospects. Then, I will do the closing. If you cannot create some prospects then; I will simply take you back to the company". Suddenly, they arrived in some housing area. Pistol came across a home, where they were having a cookout. Anthony thought great; he was confident, he could sell a box of meat to somebody here. Pistol parked his car on the curb, in front of the house.

Pistol replied, "I am going to park right here and see, just how good you are in creating a buyer. When you find an individual, who is interested in buying a box of meat then, you find me. I will get out the vehicle and do the closing. While you are doing this, I will be checking in with the company on my cell phone". Anthony starts walking towards the cookout. He was thinking; this was his last chance to prove, he can create a buyer.

Anthony kept repeating, "I can do this; this is going to be easy". He walks around cars parked in the grass. Then, he walks on a brick trail, which leads to the cookout. Anthony finds African Americans, who were socializing together, talking, smoking, and drinking by an open pit grill. They appeared to be friendly because they waved hello at him, as he was coming closer towards them. Anthony replied, "How's everybody doing? I am a meat seller and was curious if anybody would be interested in buying meat.

A guy turned and looked at him. He replied, "Sure, I am interested. Except, I would need to inspect, before I decide to buy. Anthony replied, "Well, how about you walk to the vehicle and have a look at the meat". Then, Bullet appeared from nowhere. He replied, "We are all drug dealers. We will make a swap, drugs for meat. Anthony started to recognize Bullet; as Bullet replied, "We are all drug dealers". Anthony became worried. He replied, "Wait a minute; and I will get my supervisor". Bullet and other guys followed Anthony to where Pistol's car was located.

Anthony arrived at Pistol's car. He inspected the car inside and out but; there was no Pistol. He opened the door; and the ignition key was still inside the ignition. Bullet replied, "Okay, meat-salesman. Show me where the meat is located, you are selling." Anthony replied, "It is inside the trunk". Bullet replied, "Open the trunk; and let us see, what you have". Anthony opened the trunk. Bullet replied, "Nice! We will take everything". Anthony replied, "Great but; it will cost, a lot of money". Bullet replied, "I told you, we are drug dealers. We give you drugs".

Anthony replied, "What if, I told you no. Another guy pointed his handgun at Anthony's forehead. Anthony replied, "No problem, go ahead and take the meat. I don't even care!" Bullet began laughing. He ordered the other guys to take all the meat, which was in the trunk. Then, they ordered Anthony to empty his wallet. Sadly, those guys also stole Anthony's money. Then, they departed quickly. Shortly afterward, Pistol returned. Anthony explained to Pistol; all the guys who were at the cookout, stole his money, including the meats. Pistol pretended to be upset with Anthony. He informed Anthony; Anthony would be liable for all the meats being stolen.

Pistol drove Anthony to Greensboro and stopped at some apartment complex. He walked inside an apartment. Later, a girl walked to Pistol's parked vehicle. Anthony was waiting for Pistol, patiently inside the vehicle. She presumed to advise Anthony, for him to leave and run for his life. The girl informed Anthony; she overheard Pistol say, "He was about to kill a guy, who he was training to sell meats". Pistol was inquiring information on how to hide a dead body. Anthony walked to the nearest store and called the Nebraska meat company to pick him up. The Nebraska meat company sent another worker to take Anthony back to the company.

When Anthony got back to the company, the manager ordered him into his office. The Manager replied, "I have your information on file. I noticed; you have no meat selling experience. This is the reason, why being a meat-salesman did not work out. I am sorry, for your time wasted. I will make sure; we will not be contacting you anymore for work. When Anthony decided to fill out the application for the Nebraska meat company, he only put his street address down and not his house number. Anthony had recently relocated at his current address and couldn't remember the house number by memory.

The first thing Anthony decided to do, when arriving at his home, was call Fungi. Anthony explained to him, his business associates robbed him. Anthony replied, "Your two drug dealer associates, who you advise me about the job, rob me and cause me extreme distress. In addition, now I owe the meat manager over $250 dollars in meats presumably stolen". Fungi could tell, Anthony was very unhappy.

Fungi replied, "You don't have to worry. I will pay Pistol and Bullet back from all the hardships, they have caused you".

Fungi figured; by next week, he would have a business proposition to make with Pistol and Bullet. After he makes this deal, there want to be a need for money anymore. This will be payback to Pistol and Bullet, from what they have caused. As a result, Pistol and Bullet created killings of innocent people because of the drug exchange deal between Fungi and them. It started with an innocent drug exchange deal, ending with revenge, confusion and death. With the conclusion of my daughter A.K.A Half Pint, or as I call her Keke, who became involved right in the middle of things.

After Fungi stole Pistol and Bullet drug money, Pistol and Bullet killed Fungi, while trying to recover their drug money. Furthermore, what they realize, Fungi did not have their briefcase with the drug money. Pistol and Bullet decided to look for Anthony. Although, they had one problem. Pistol and Bullet did not know, where Anthony's home address was really located. All they had was a street address from their supervisor. In retaliation, Pistol and Bullet kidnap Anthony's daughter Keke at a college football game, in order to regain the briefcase full of drug money.

Pistol and Bullet began riding around town with Keke in the back seat. Bullet begins telling Keke, "Don't be afraid, we are just going for a little joy ride. I hope you enjoy car rides". Keke replied, "Yeah!" Pistol replied, "Who wants to be cooped up at a football stadium, watching men run around crazy, and chasing for a funny shaped ball. Pistol and I are going to take you to the club. Then, we will meet our supervisor. Next, we are going to get our briefcase full of money". Pistol drove them to a secluded club in Rural Hall, about a 10-minute drive away.

Once they reached the club in Rural Hall, everyone inside the vehicle exited the automobile. Then, they entered the nightclub. Bullet escorted Keke through the front entrance. When everyone finally entered, a strange gentleman motion them to a round table. The gentleman was the manager of Nebraska meat delivery. He alerted the waiter for assistance. Then, the manager replied, "Waiter, please give my guess, whatever they would like to drink". Bullet replied, "Okay, pretty lady, what can we get you to drink". The waiter replied, "Here is a menu".

Keke looked at the menu. She replied, "Oh, I will take this one; this one also, and this one too". Then, Bullet replied, "Wow, she is thirsty! The meat manager replied, "Go ahead, I don't care. Get her what she wants because this is Anthony's daughter". Pistol replied, "Yes, this is right! I learned about him a little bit". The waiter returns with everybody's drinks. Keke instantly begins sipping her drink. Keke replied, "Turn the music up". Everyone else in the club, who is listening, begins to laugh.

The manager replied, "This is good, I am glad. We are all happy because we have some insurance. Now, Anthony will want to cooperate with us on our demands. Call Anthony on his cell phone and notify him, we have his daughter. I am sure; he will be very interested to know, how to retrieve his daughter. Keke smacks the meat manager on his thigh. Bullet was shocked. He replied, "I apologize for this Sir". Keke replied, "I said, turn the music up! If not, I am going to smack you". The meat manager looked at Keke strangely.

The manager replied, "She is alright, isn't she?" Pistol replied, "I believe, she is a special needs person. She is not in her right mind". Bullet replied, "She better be out of her right mind, for smacking the manager on his thigh". Pistol replied, "Sorry boss man, I will handle her". Keke replied, "I am sorry. I want do it no more". Bullet replied, "You better not!" Keke walked over to the manager to apologize. Pistol grabbed Keke by the hand and pull her towards him. Bullet replied, "Little girl, this will be enough showing out now! You sit down and behave yourself".

Bullet pulls his gun out and points it at Keke. Pistol replied, "Bullet don't! I have control over her. I say again; she is not in her right mind. She is a special needs person". Bullet replied, "Well, you better take care of her, before I shoot her". Pistol picks up Keke with one hand and carries her on to the dance floor. Keke starts shouting the entire time while saying, "No, put me down!" Pistol begins dancing with Keke to calm her nerves. The meat manager replied, "Hey, Bullet call Anthony right now; while he can retrieve his daughter. Tell him to bring us our money".

Prior to Bullet informing Anthony on his cell phone; Anthony investigates Pistol and Bullets residence. When Anthony arrives at the residence, there is a yard sale on the side area of the residence. Anthony has his co-worker Mark, as an assistant riding on the passenger side inside his vehicle. Mark exits the vehicle and begin hunting for Keke. An elderly woman in charge are selling household goods at the yard sale. Mark asked the elderly woman for the location of Pistol and Bullet. The elderly woman inquired; why he wanted to know this information? Mark replied, "These men have my co-worker's daughter".

The elderly woman promises Mark, she would give him the location of Pistol and Bullet; only if he comes inside the residence and look at more items for sale. Mark agrees with the elderly lady; and the elderly lady escorts Mark inside the residence. As Mark enters through the front door, gangsters were waiting with weapons. The gangsters demand Mark to handover his wallet. Mark begged for mercy on his life. Mark informs; go ahead take my wallet but spare me my life.

Simultaneously, Anthony sits in the vehicle patiently for Mark to return. Anthony witnesses an elderly lady with Mark. Then, 2 gangsters enter the residence. The 2 gangsters resembled Pistol and Bullet so; Anthony walked to the front door and touched the doorbell. An elderly lady answered the door. Anthony replied, "Please, help me because Pistol and Bullet have my daughter! Please, help me". The elderly lady replied, "I know you! You helped my daughter Ethel become a homeowner. Now, my granddaughter has become a straight-A student in school".

Anthony informed the elderly lady; my friend is a Caucasian guy. His name is Mark, and he is my co-worker looking for my missing daughter. Please, don't hurt him. Then, Anthony's phone rings. Anthony answered his phone. He hears Bullet's voice. Anthony whispered, "It's Bullet!" The elderly lady placed her index finger to her lips. She whispered, "Hang up the phone. I will help you find them". Anthony placed his cell phone to his ear and listened. Bullet replied, "I know, you are on the phone listening. If you want your special needs daughter alive, you better communicate with me".

CHAPTER 9
NO FAIR EXCHANGE

Bullet informed; he knows I have his drug money. He is hanging up the phone but; I better call him whenever I can talk. Your daughter's life is in your hands so, call me by this phone number". Anthony slowly disconnected the phone and put it in his pocket. He informed Mark; this ordeal is not going to be solved in one night. Thanks for your help but; it is getting late now. Please don't notify the police. I will tell my job, I am sick. Anthony understood now; his livelihood was in great danger.

Anthony figured; because of Fungi's involvement with a drug deal exchange, was the cause for his death. It was also why; his daughter was kidnap and all this drama was occurring. Anthony was in real trouble. He must go home and confess to his wife, what he believes is true. Anthony went home and confessed to his wife Pricilla. Pricilla replied, "I cannot believe, you are telling me, somebody has kidnapped our daughter. I have been telling you, Fungi was a bad friend from the start. You were determined to be friends with Fungi. Now, you must go and get our daughter back. Go settle Fungi affairs with these drug dealers".

Pricilla's house phone rings; and she picks up the phone. When she answers it, Angela from Georgia was on the receiving end. Pricilla replied, "Hey cousin, how you are doing?" Tyrone and you are here. You all are in our driveway right now. That's wonderful, I will open the front door for you all". Pricilla opens the front door; and Angela walks through the front entrance. Tyrone comes in behind Angela with luggage for a weekend visit. Anthony replied, "Welcome everybody, anyone needs my assistance with anything else".

Anthony helped carry additional items into the house, while Pricilla stayed inside. As Anthony was outside, the next-door neighbor was working in his front yard. The neighbor observed Anthony's visitors. His name was Stroman; and he stopped to introduce himself to Anthony's out of town guest. Stroman replied, "Hello Anthony. I see, you have guest. Sorry for the intrusion. Anthony replied, "No problem. I want to introduce you to my cousin-in-law Tyrone and his wife Angela. They are inside the house, talking to Pricilla".

Simultaneously while Mr. Stroman got introduced to Angela and Tyrone, Mr. Stroman replied, "I am happy to meet you all. The reason for my visit is because a strange occurrence is happening in our neighborhood. I heard gunfire this morning, as I was walking down the street. In the process, I called to report it to the police. There were screams and a lot of pleading in the background distance at this house on the street corner of Whitfield Rd". Anthony replied, "You said, a lot of screams?"

Stroman replied, "Yes, I wonder did anybody else hear it. It was strange. There was a lot of pleading. The victim replied, 'Please, don't shoot! I don't know, who you are looking for. I cannot help you find the child's father; and I don't know nothing about a briefcase full of money'. Then, I heard a little girl's voice. She replied, 'I want my daddy!' The voice sounds familiar but; I can't distinguish it at this moment".

Stroman informed; I kept remembering the victim saying, "I don't know, where your daddy is located little girl". Finally, I heard more gun shots; and a little girl's voice saying "No!" This was when; I noticed two men walking with a little girl in the far distance. I just rushed to call the police and now, I find out our neighbor has been shot and killed. Anthony replied, "It could have been a family incident. They say, more deaths come from domestic abuse. Tyrone looked at the neighbor strangely and shook his head. He replied, "I have heard the same thing".

Stroman replied, "I have not heard of any crime related events in this area before. I have lived here in the neighborhood for a long time. This is the first time; I have heard of a murder on my street. I take pride in being the neighborhood watchdog around here. For this to happen here, sickens my stomach. If you all good neighbors hear about any evidence of the killers, notify me or the police. I will keep you inform of any issues going on. Goodbye and stay safe now".

Tyrone looked at Anthony and replied, "How are your children?" Anthony replied, "Funtasia is in college doing fine. Half Pint, I hate to say. You know how your Half Pint does. Well, it's a long story. A long bad story. I got to tell you. I am in trouble. Big trouble happened to me because of my friend. Some drug dealers kidnapped our Keke!" Tyrone looked puzzled. He replied, "How did you allow some drug dealers to steal your daughter. Please don't tell me. They got Half Pint!" Anthony stood beside Tyrone to comfort him. He explained the entire situation to Tyrone.

Anthony also explained to Tyrone; he couldn't confide with the police because he could get arrested for knowledge of a drug exchange dealing, happening with his friend. As the day was turning into night, Tyrone and Anthony decided to end the day by informing their wives; how they were going to search for Tequila. Pricilla and Angela notified local people about a kidnapping. An abduction of Keke, who was a special needs person, would require a mass neighborhood watch effort to find her location.

Suddenly, there was a ringing sound from the house phone. It was an insurance man for Pricilla. The insurance man notified; he will be in the area, planning to do a routine check. Pricilla notified to the insurance man; she had a lot of unfortunate circumstances occurring all at one time. If possible, could he come at another time. The insurance man replied, "You, don't have to worry. I will only come and observe the area by walk through. Then, if everything is fine, I will only need you to sign the documents for the insurance".

Pricilla replied, "If this is extremely necessary and then, okay". When the next morning arrived, Tyrone and Anthony decided to take a walk up the street in the neighborhood. The next-door neighbor Stroman was watering his grass. He observed Tyrone and Anthony standing outside. Stroman replied, "Hey neighbors, I found out some information today. The killers are returning to our neighborhood. They are drug dealers, who are looking for drug money".

Stroman informed; the killers have been making death threat statements. The killers replied, "They have killed one person. If they don't get their drug money then, they will kill others. Bad things are going to keep on happening unless they get their drug money". Stroman replied, "This is bad. We have never had this much problems in this neighborhood. They are going to kill the whole entire neighborhood. We got murderers, drug dealers and now, kidnappers looking for drug money. What has our neighborhood become too? Where are the police, when you need them?"

With face turning red, Stroman returned to his property. Tyrone replied, "You got drug dealers in this neighborhood. I wonder, who would be crazy enough to steal a drug dealer's money in this neighborhood. This neighborhood is too nice for this. I believe the drug dealers have made a mistake. I presume Anthony, we need to investigate the situation up the road. I hope, you are not afraid to investigate with me. Anthony, you don't have to worry because I will protect you. I always keep myself strapped. Tyrone lifts his coat up and showed a 45-caliber pistol strapped on his side.

Anthony replied, "Oh, you don't have to worry about me. I have weapons of mass destruction. With killers on the loose, I have a

38-caliber handgun for my protection and a M60 machine gun for my family's protection". Tyrone replied, "How did you get a machine gun?" Anthony replied, "I have my connections because it is always best to be prepared". He opened his garage door and besides his truck being parked, a M60 machine gun was resting inside his garage with military uniforms. Tyrone replied, "The handgun is idea but; the machine gun needs to stay hidden. We are not fighting an army here"

Anthony replied, "I have just moved into this area. Already, I am experiencing crime". Tyrone replied, "I guess, whatever area you live in, it doesn't matter because crime happens everywhere". Inside Anthony's house, Pricilla and Angela are conveying while drinking coffee. Pricilla decided to look out the window. She observed Anthony and Tyrone leaving the property. Angela replied, "It is beautiful outside". Pricilla replied, "Yes, it is because our husbands has decided to take a walk in the neighborhood". Angela replied, "My husband does this a lot to ease our stress".

Angela informed Pricilla; probably Tyrone has persuaded Anthony to walk in the neighborhood to ease the stress as well. Angela replied, "Tyrone and I feel, Half Pint is in the neighborhood somewhere. I bet, there is a neighbor, who knows something about Half Pint and will give us information. We have to be persistent with finding them". Angela also informed Pricilla; I found a black briefcase on your guest bed. In return, I moved it out the way. I am giving it to you". Pricilla replied, "Thanks!" Pricilla examined the briefcase in curiosity and opened it up. The briefcase had money stored inside. The money was worth a half million dollars.

Pricilla notified Anthony by cell phone of the money stored inside the briefcase. Anthony informed Tyrone; unknowingly, his wife found the drug dealer's money in a briefcase at his house. Now, he needs to contact the drug dealers, in order to get his daughter back. As Tyrone and Anthony are returning home, they observed a house with a police officer posted at its front door. The front door had a lot of bullet holes inside. An ambulance arrived simultaneously. Anthony replied, "How are you doing, officer?" Tyrone replied, "Hello, Officer Sir. We would like to know, what is happening here?"

Police officer replied, "If you don't know by now, killings are happening in this area. If you all are walking in the area on foot, you must be extremely careful. Killers are on the lookout for a briefcase full of drug money. If anyone has helpful information, notify me Officer Ray. Here is my business card". Tyrone replied, "Thank you, Mr. Officer". Officer Ray then, received a radio call of another invasion in the area. The invasion was one block down from there area on Whitfield St. The report came from Mr. Stroman, the neighborhood watchman.

Anthony listened to the complaint address. It was coming from Mr. Stroman's address. Anthony informed Tyrone; it is my neighbor's house which is being burglarized. We must move quickly to make it back home. Anthony and Tyrone decided to rush home to give Mr. Stroman assistance, Angela is observing the view at Anthony's house through the kitchen window. Angela replied, "Pricilla, you do have a nice backyard. The grass is so pretty; and the flowers are blooming so bright". Then, a stranger began walking through the backyard. He was really enjoying the view".

Angela replied, "A stranger is in the backyard." Pricilla replied, "Where?" Angela replied, "The stranger is walking everywhere in your backyard and looking at the house". Pricilla rushes to the kitchen window. She replied, "I do see a strange man and my neighbor Mr. Stroman". Mr. Stroman was out there to greet the stranger with a cell phone in his hand. Now, a policeman arrived, talking to them with handcuffs in his hand. The neighbor Mr. Stroman was pointing his finger at the stranger. The policeman decided to take the stranger away in handcuffs". Angela replied, "You think, this might be the drug dealer".

Pricilla replied, "I sure hope, it was the drug dealer so; all this mess can be over with finally". Angela replied, "Now, maybe we can get our Half Pint back home". Tyrone and Anthony hastily arrived at

Anthony's home. They found a police car departing from Anthony's neighbor's house with a victim handcuffed and carrying a briefcase. Mr. Stroman waves at the police car, as it drives away. Anthony replied, "Mr. Stroman, what happened?"

Mr. Stroman replied, "I got him. The guy was snooping in your backyard". Tyrone replied, "You got who?". Mr. Stroman replied, "I got the drug dealer. He had the briefcase and everything". Anthony replied, "This is great! How about my daughter? Did you see her too?" Mr. Stroman replied, "Nope, I am sorry". Anthony replied, "This means somebody still has my daughter". Mr. Stroman replied, "What, somebody still has your daughter?" Anthony replied, "Yes! There is still at least, another drug dealer on the loose. They have my daughter".

Tyrone replied, "This means Anthony, our job is not complete. We are going to tell our wives, we are still out here looking, for the drug dealers and Half Pint. I got a feeling; Half Pint is around here somewhere in the neighborhood". Tyrone and Anthony walked in the house. Pricilla replied, "I have some good news. They have the drug dealer". Anthony replied, "They have someone but; whomever has Keke was still loose on the move. Pistol was a tall slender man. Bullet was a plump and medium built guy". Angela replied, "You know these men. Then, finding Half Pint should be easy".

Tyrone replied, "It will be easy if they are roaming in the neighborhood. Anthony and I are going to do another sweep of the area. We should find something this time. Don't worry, we will find Half Pint and put an end to this drama". Tyrone and Anthony continued with the search for Half Pint and the drug dealer. 2 police officers escorted the suspected stranger as the drug dealer to the City Police Station for questioning. The questioning suspect was verbally shouting, "This is a mistake! Police Officers, you got the wrong person," while he spoke to the police officer driving the police car.

Next, the questioning suspect claimed; he was an insurance man. The suspect mention, "he was only there to do a routine home inspection for a client named Pricilla to receive insurance". He admitted; his client was notified of the arranged visit ahead of time. Unfortunately, an overreacted neighbor concluded, he was a burglar and a drug dealer. Then, the neighbor decided to inform the police. The suspect advised the police; he will notify his company. His company will clear him of the misunderstanding. The policeman replied, "We don't care! I know how, you drug dealers operate".

The police officer made a conscience objective to do a drive by, around all the homes which were burglarized and who had a show of incidents by drug dealers in the past week. He wanted the neighbors on Whitfield Rd. to observe, the Winston-Salem Police Department had captured a suspect in the drug dealing crimes. When the police officer made a left turn on White St. to exit off Whitfield Rd., they proceeded to the police station. As the police officer turned on White St., they passed Bullet, Pistol, and Keke hiding behind a bushy area.

Pistol replied, "Bullet, I think this was a great idea to park the car around the block and walk the rest of the way". Bullet replied, "Yes, it was". As they begin to walk towards Whitfield Rd., they observed Anthony and Tyrone leaving a residence on foot. Bullet replied, "Pistol, I see Anthony and some other guy leaving a residence. This must be Anthony's home". Keke replied, "There goes my daddy and Cousin Tyrone leaving home". Pistol replied, "This is your home". Bullet replied, "Quickly! Everyone finds a hiding place to hide. We can hide behind this house across the street from them".

CHAPTER 10
KILLER, KILLER, KILLER

nthony and Tyrone walked down the driveway into the street. Then, they made a right turn down Whitfield Rd. They by-pass Pistol, Bullet, and Keke hiding behind an abandon house across the street. When Tyrone and Anthony could not be located anymore, Bullet informed; the close is clear. Bullet replied, "This is my chance to enter Anthony's house and retrieve the briefcase full of money. Later, we can get rid of the little girl". Pistol replied, "This is going to be sad. It was fun knowing her. I began feeling a little sympathy for her".

Bullet replied, "Alright Pistol, I want you to stay put with the girl. I will head down to Anthony's house and peep through the window and see if anybody is there. If, I don't see anybody, I will break in". Bullet walks to Anthony's house and peeps in through a window. Angela was simultaneously, looking out the same window. Angela was startled by Bullet. She screamed, "Pricilla, there is another stranger in your backyard". Pricilla replied, "I am coming to see, who it is". Pricilla noticed a man, medium built looking, who appeared dressed for business. She figured; this must be the insurance man. He cannot be the drug dealer because he looked like a professional businessman.

Pricilla notified Angela; the close is clear because it is the insurance man. She opened the door and informed; Bullet to come inside her home. Bullet replied, "Well, good evening. I can tell, you have been expecting me. I would like to know if you have the money?" Pricilla replied, "Fantastic, I am approved this fast". Bullet replied, "Approved? Oh, yes sure. You are certainly approved". I am going to notify my company; everything is good so far. Bullet notified Pistol; he could proceed with bringing their package to the front door.

He requested Pricilla to bring him the money. Pricilla replied, "Wonderful, I will call my husband on his cell phone about the good news". Bullet replied, "This is not necessary. I just need the briefcase please. Then, I will give you, your package". Angela replied, "I suspect, you are not the insurance man.?" Bullet replied, "No, I am not the insurance man! Although, we both collect money. This is the only thing; I have in common with an insurance salesman. I would rather be a drug dealer or a killer. Now, please hand me the briefcase". Pricilla replied, "What if, I refused to give you the briefcase".

Bullet replied, "My brother will kill your daughter, if you refuse me because he has a gun". Angela replied, "Okay, I will get the briefcase for you, Sir". As these events were happening, Anthony and Tyrone took a break from walking. Anthony spotted a red Camaro, a block up the road. Anthony replied, "This is Pistol car. He might be on our street somewhere. I will call my wife to notify her". Tyrone replied, "Don't bother, I will call mines". As Tyrone attempts to notify his wife, her phone was off. Tyrone replied, "My wife cell phone is off. This is a distress sign. There is a problem at your house".

Tyrone and Anthony rushed back to Anthony's home. Anthony called the police to notify them; possible killers or drug dealers are on the loose in the neighborhood at his address. The police officer already verified through an insurance company; the questionable suspect obtained was an insurance man on an appointment. The suspect was not a drug dealer. When Tyrone and Anthony reached Anthony's home, they find Pistol holding Keke's hand in the front yard. Mr. Stroman, who was outside in his front yard, noticed a man with Keke in the driveway. He notified the police officer of the situation.

Mr. Stroman informed the police; please come quickly. I believe, there is going to be trouble. The police officer replied, "We have been informed and are proceeding to the area". Anthony and Tyrone crept to Anthony's house with caution. As they approached slowly closer to Pistol and Keke; Anthony's front door opened. Angela and Pricilla slowly walked out first. Then, Bullet had a handgun in one hand and the briefcase in his other hand, as he walked behind them. Bullet noticed; Anthony and Tyrone approaching the house.

Bullet replied, "You are too late, Anthony! Pistol should have killed you, when you were trying to sell meat. I should have killed you". Now, I have my briefcase, full of money. I am sorry but; we have to kill your family and you too". Anthony replied, "You are going to kill my family? My family don't have nothing to do with this". Pistol replied, "We have our money now; we don't need to kill anybody else. We are good now Bullet". Bullet replied, "I don't care about his family or his special needs daughter. They all must die, starting with his stupid daughter".

Pistol replied, "You are wrong Bullet. I told you, she is not stupid. She is special. Don't talk about her this way. I have sympathy for her; and nobody is going to harm her". Bullet replied, "I know, you are not going to botch this job up, over a stupid dumb child. I order you, little brother to shoot her. Right now!" Pistol replied, "Nobody is going to shoot her. If you want to kill the rest of her family. Then, go ahead! Furthermore, my little girlfriend is going to live". Bullet replied, "All right, if you don't want to pull the trigger and kill her. Then, I will do it".

Bullet pointed his handgun at Anthony. Keke replied, "No, not my daddy!" Keke jumped in front of Anthony. Bullet pulls the trigger of his handgun, instantly shooting Keke. Keke falls to the ground.

Anthony was in disbelief, as everyone else was. He cannot believe Keke has been shot and not him. Anthony tried to come to his daughter's aide but; Pistol assisted to Keke's aide quicker. Bullet replied, "Pistol let her go". Pistol replied, "You meant to do this. Bullet, you are going to pay for this". Pistol pulls his handgun out quickly and shoots Bullet.

After Pistol shoots Bullet, Bullet goes down; and Pistol turns around to assist Keke again. Anthony replied, "Pistol, let her go. I can handle her. Pistol continues assisting Keke. Tyrone replied, "Her father said leave her alone". Pistol continued assisting Keke. Tyrone pulled his 45-caliber pistol out and shoots Pistol in the back. Pistol falls directly on top of Keke. Anthony replied, "Tyrone hold your fire". Tyrone replied, "Oops! I am sorry. I figured; he was going to hurt Keke even more". As Pistol moved over beside Keke, he touches her face.

Pistol replied, "I love you, baby girl". Keke opens her eyes. She replied, "I love you, baby girl". Pistol starts laughing in a soft voice. He replied, "You are going to be okay." Keke replied, "You are going to be okay." Keke rubs Pistol face to comfort him. Pistol closes his eyes and passes away. The police officers arrived with the ambulance. They inquired was anybody hurt. Anthony replied, "Yes! My daughter has a bullet wound but; I think, she is going to be alright. She is talking. The guy beside her named Pistol, I think, he is dead. I have no clue about this guy over here, named Bullet".

The medics put Keke in an ambulance with Pricilla, in one vehicle. Behind them, Pistol was placed in another vehicle. Bullet was in a separate ambulance. Anthony and Tyrone rode inside a police car for questioning and to fill out criminal reports. Angela monitored Anthony's house, while everyone else was gone. The neighbor Mr. Stroman wrote his own recollection of the incident for the cops and kept a good neighborhood watch for the rest of the area. The incident lasted an entire week, starting with Fungi's death and until Keke's recapture by her parents.

In the process, over a dozen close neighbors were affected by harm or death. Anthony gave statements to the police of the drug money and what he knew about the drug dealers. Eventually, hospitalization was able to restore Keke health back to normalcy. Tyrone and Angela traveled back to Georgia. Pricilla was accepted for life insurance and lived a healthier drug free life. Anthony continued working but kept his M60 machine gun and pistol loaded for any more killer drug dealers, who might turn the neighborhood into a killing spree.

Bullet was committed to a jail, at a maximum prison facility in Raleigh, NC. Everything, final got back to normal again. Anthony was content. Then, a year passed away since the incident. A heavy-set man visited Anthony's house. He was shouting, "Fresh meat for sale, at a low discount price. I have steak, pork, and seafood. The voice and sales pitch sounded very familiar to Anthony. It was Tony, the meat salesman. Tony was in a Nebraska Meat sales truck. Before Anthony could reach the door, Pricilla was there to greet the salesman.

Pricilla replied, "Would this be the best sales pitch, a Nebraska Meat salesperson got?" Tony replied, "I am one of the best salesmen in the area". Pricilla replied, "You know, it is very disrespectful to be shouting at someone's front door. I tell you, what I will do for you. Anthony show the man, how you sell something". Anthony walked to the front door. Anthony replied, "You are the Nebraska Meat salesman. Well! It's two things, you should always be familiar with. A pistol and a bullet; now, leave before one finds you!"

'THE END'

TO THE PURCHASER

Thank You for Purchasing Killer, Killer, Killer and The Drug Exchange Dealer.

Other Travel2Treasure novels include: Cousin in Love, U-Turn to Cousin in Love, Children's Cherokee Indian Carnival and the Ghoul. Soon to be written: The Vintage House and many others. All support will be greatly appreciated to fund Travel2Treasure novels by Charles Anthony Jackson.

REMARKS

Princerena Jackson (Deceased Wife) -God Bless
Chontaye Jackson (Daughter) – big shouts
Tequila Jackson (Daughter) – big shouts
Deborah Jackson (Mother) -big shouts
Richard Jackson (Father) – big shouts
Bobby Jackson (Brother) – big shouts
Felise Lawson (Sister in Law) – big shouts
Rodney Lawson (Brother in Law) – big shouts
City of Winston-Salem, NC – big shouts
City of Gray, Ga – big shouts
Book Publishers – big shouts
Finally – GOD – big shouts